'You'll never find whatever the hell it is you're looking for until you stop running, James. Do you even know what it is any more?'

Good question. What did he want? He'd got away from the sadness of his earlier life, but was he any happier? Didn't he want to be happy? To be loved and feel needed? All the things he hadn't had in his younger years.

But what if he stuffed up? It was easier to move on than risk his heart again.

'It's a good life,' he said defensively, as his head roared with conflicting emotions.

'Have you ever thought maybe there's a flipside to your life that's just as good?'

He'd more than thought it. He'd been living the flipside here in this cottage in Skye with her, and he liked it more than he cared to admit.

'You shouldn't let your past stuff up a shot at the future either,' she continued. 'So let's start again. Let's make our own family. Let me be your family.'

Amy Andrews has always loved writing, and still can't quite believe that she gets to do it for a living. Creating wonderful heroines and gorgeous heroes and telling their stories is an amazing way to pass the day. Sometimes they don't always act as she'd like them to, but then neither do her kids, so she's kind of used to it. Amy lives in the very beautiful Samford Valley, with her husband and aforementioned children, along with six brown chooks and two black dogs. She loves to hear from her readers. Drop her a line at www.amyandrews.com.au

Recent titles by the same author:

FOUND: A FATHER FOR HER CHILD
THE ITALIAN COUNT'S BABY
SINGLE DAD, OUTBACK WIFE
AN UNEXPECTED PROPOSAL

THE OUTBACK DOCTOR'S SURPRISE BRIDE

BY
AMY ANDREWS

MILLS & BOON™

Pure reading pleasure

All the characters in this book have no existence outside the imagination of the author, and have no relation whatsoever to anyone bearing the same name or names. They are not even distantly inspired by any individual known or unknown to the author, and all the incidents are pure invention.

First published in Great Britain 2008
Harlequin Mills & Boon Limited,
Eton House, 18-24 Paradise Road, Richmond, Surrey TW9 1SR

© Amy Andrews 2008

ISBN: 978 0 263 86323 9

Set in Times Roman 10½ on 12¾ pt
03-0508-47350

Printed and bound in Spain
by Litografia Rosés, S.A., Barcelona

THE OUTBACK DOCTOR'S SURPRISE BRIDE

To my sister-in-law Jeanette for reading all my books.
Thank you, your support means so much.

CHAPTER ONE

DR JAMES REMINGTON flipped open his visor as he sped down the arrow-straight highway. He revelled in the power of the vintage Harley engine growling between his legs, the air on his cheeks and the way the softening light of the encroaching dusk blanketed the thick bush in its ghostly splendour.

He raised his face to the sky and let out a long joyous whoop, his gypsy heart singing. This was the life. The open road. The sun on your face. The wind at your back. Freedom. He felt a surge of pleasure rise in his chest as a familiar affinity with the environment enveloped him. He felt a part of the land.

A solitary road sign appeared in the distance, announcing Skye, his destination, was only five kilometres away. It loomed large and then was gone in the blink of an eye. He felt anticipation heighten his senses. On a deeper level an unwanted thought intruded. Maybe this time he'd find what he was looking for. A place to hang up his helmet. A place to call home.

He shook his head to quell the ridiculous childhood longing. The wind was on his face, he had freedom—why did he need roots? The township of Skye was just another outback stop in the many he'd made in the last few years. And after Skye there'd be another and then another until he reached the Cape and then he'd…figure out his next move then.

The road started to twist and turn a little as it wended its way through thick stands of gumtrees and heavy bush. James eased back on his speed as he leant into the curves, enjoying the zigzag of the powerful bike.

He rounded a bend and came face to face with his worst nightmare. His headlights caught the silhouettes of several cows meandering across the highway in the waning light. He had seconds to respond. He braked and swerved and in the split second before his bike slid out from underneath him and he was catapulted across the tar, James knew that, whatever happened next, it wasn't going to be good.

Helen Franklin was annoyed. It was nine p.m. She'd been hanging around for a couple of hours, waiting for the locum doctor to arrive. Had he arrived? No. His bags had arrived by courier earlier but he was still a no-show. The casserole she'd cooked for him sat uneaten in the fridge.

She could be at the Drovers' Arms, joining in the weekly trivia night. Her team was at the top of the table and she hated missing it. She'd tried phoning his mobile number the agency had furnished her with a few times but had had no response. Not that that necessarily meant anything. Mobile phone reception out here was dodgy at best between towns and only marginally better in them.

An uneasy feeling bunched the muscles at her neck and she hoped some catastrophe hadn't befallen him. But as he was only two hours late she doubted she'd manage to convince anyone to send out a search party for him. No, she just had to wait and hope that he showed or at least rang in to explain.

He'd probably just changed his mind about coming to Skye and hadn't bothered to tell anyone. Country towns were notoriously hard to attract medical staff to. She'd had a request in for a locum since Genevieve had announced her pregnancy and she was now thirty-six weeks gone.

Well, damn it all, she wasn't going to hang around all night, waiting, when the new doctor couldn't even be bothered to let her know of his delay. He'd better be here by the start of business tomorrow, though. Genevieve should have given up work a month ago. Her blood pressure was borderline and her ankles were starting to swell. She needed the break. She'd admitted only yesterday that she was completely exhausted by lunchtime most days.

Helen left a terse note on the dining-room table, gathered her stuff and left, pulling the door closed behind her. There was no need for a key. This was Skye. Nobody locked their doors. And when she saw him in the morning, she was going to give Dr James Remington a piece of her mind, and if that set the tone with her flatmate for the next four months then so be it.

James woke to birdsong and the first rays of sunlight stabbing at his closed lids. The pain in his right leg grabbed at him again and he gritted his teeth. He felt like hell. He'd had a fitful night's sleep on the hard ground. He was hungry, his bladder was full and his mouth tasted as if an insect had crawled inside during the night and died there.

His broken leg throbbed unmercilessly despite the splint he'd managed to fashion from the branch of a tree. At least it was daylight now. His hopes of rescue had improved dramatically. He looked at his watch. He was now twelve hours past his ETA—surely someone would be worrying?

All he had to do was get himself to the roadside and hope that the highway to Skye was busier during the day than it had been during the long hours he'd lain in the dark. He'd only heard two vehicles all night. The bitumen was probably only a few metres or so away, but he knew just from the small amount of moving he'd done after the accident that with his broken leg, it was going to feel like a kilometre by the time he'd got there.

He'd decided against moving too far last night. Dusk had turned to darkness quickly and visibility had been a problem. The night was impossibly black out here, the bush incredibly thick. Through a mammoth effort he'd managed to drag himself over to his nearby bike. He hadn't been able to see it and had had to rely on his sense of hearing, heading towards the sound of the still running engine.

Thirty minutes later he'd been sweating with effort and the excruciating pain of every bump jolting through his injured leg. He'd pulled his torch out of his bike's tote bag and located some paltry first-aid supplies to help him with his leg. He'd had his swag and some water and with his mobile phone showing no reception, he'd known he was there till the morning.

As tempting as it had been to push himself, he had known it would be sensible to wait for daylight. Apart from his leg and some minor scratches, he'd escaped re-markably uninjured so the last thing he'd needed had been to reach the road and then be run over by an unsuspecting car. He was in black leathers and a black T-shirt. Even his hair was black. He had hardly been the most visible thing in the inky outback night.

James relieved himself with difficulty and with one final look back at his bike gritted his teeth and began the slow arduous crawl through the bush to the road.

Helen woke to the ringing phone just before six a.m. and was dismayed to find the spare bedroom not slept in and the note she'd left last night untouched on the table. She'd come home from the pub to an empty house but had hoped the missing locum had crept in during the night.

She answered the phone tersely, preparing to give James Remington a good lecture. But it was only Elsie and she spent ten minutes listening to the latest calamity before she was able to get off the phone. *Damn it!* James Remington had better have a good excuse for his tardiness.

A feeling of unease crept over her again and she quickly punched in the local policeman's number.

His sleepy voice answered. 'Sorry, Reg, it's Helen. I know it's early. I hope I didn't wake you.'

'It's fine. What's up?'

'The new doctor still hasn't shown. Have there been any accident reports?'

'Not that I know of. Do you think something's happened?'

'Not sure.'

'I'm sure he's fine, Helen. Like I said last night, he's probably just been delayed.'

'Probably,' she agreed, thinking dark thoughts about their new locum.

'He'd have to be missing for at least twenty-four hours before we could mount an official investigation.'

'I know.'

'But if you're worried I can start making some enquiries straight away. I can take the patrol car down the highway a bit.'

Helen pursed her lips, unsure. She knew Reg was probably right but she couldn't shake a nagging sense of unease. 'No, it's OK. I'm off to Elsie's now. Some of their stock broke through a fence last night and she's all het up. I'll keep my eyes peeled. I'll ring later if I still haven't heard from him.'

She rang off and looked around the empty house. *You'd better be in a ditch or laid low by a severe illness, James Remington, because this is just plain rude.*

James grunted as he inched himself slowly closer on his bottom. His movements were awkward, like a dyslexic crab. His arms were behind him, his left leg, bent at the knee, was used to push himself backward as his right leg slowly dragged against the ground as it followed.

The morning sun wasn't even high in the sky yet and he was sweating profusely. Although his leathers contributed, it was pain that caused moisture to bead above his lip and on his forehead. Every movement was agony, his leg protesting the slightest advance. He'd have given anything for a painkiller.

At just about halfway there he lay back to rest for a moment, the road now in sight. A silver car flashed by and he raised his hand and yelled out in the vain hope that he was spotted. Of course, it was futile—he was still that little bit too far away to be detected.

But he was slightly cheered by the presence of traffic. All he had to do was get the rest of the way and wait for the next car to come along.

Helen left Elsie's still distracted by their missing locum. The Desmond farm was on the outskirts of Skye and her little silver car knew the way intimately. Helen had lived with Elsie and her family on and off most of her life, permanently from the age of twelve after her mother's death.

Her mother's mental health had always been fragile, necessitating numerous hospital admissions, and her gypsy father, overwhelmed by his wife's problems and gutted by her eventual demise, had been ill equipped to care for his daughter. He'd flitted in and out of Skye as the whim had taken him, leaving Elsie to raise her.

And she had, providing stability and a much-needed loving home despite the fact that she had also been raising Duncan and Rodney, her grandsons, after their father—Elsie's son—and mother had been killed in a car accident. Duncan, who had stayed in Skye to run the farm, was the same age as Helen and they were still close.

At eighty, Elsie was a much-loved part of the family. She still lived at the homestead and now Duncan's children were benefiting from Elsie's love and eternal patience. Unfortunately in the last couple of years Elsie's health had started to fail and things that once would never have bothered her now weighed on her mind.

More often than not, when she was in a state, it was

Helen she phoned. Duncan was busy with the farm and Denise with the kids and Helen never minded. It was the least she could do for a woman who had helped her through some of the darkest times of her life.

She knew that half an hour of chit-chat and a good cup of tea soon put Elsie right. How often had Elsie taken the time to allay Helen's own fears as she'd lain awake at night, scared about the future? Elsie's hugs and calm, crackly voice had soothed her anxieties and had always loosened the knot that had seemed to be permanently present in her stomach. Easing the old woman's own fears now was never a hardship.

Helen put thoughts of Elsie aside as she concentrated on the road. Her eyes scanned either side and checked the rear-view mirror frequently. Just in case.

James mopped at his face with his bandana. He was nearly there. So close. He could hear a car approaching from a good distance away and he tried to move the last few metres quickly. Pain tore through his leg and halted his desperate movements. He swore out loud as he realised by the sound of the rapidly approaching engine he wasn't going to make it in time for this car.

In a final act of desperation he stuck up his arm and frantically waved the red bandana, even though he could tell the car had already passed. He lay back and bellowed in frustration.

Helen's gaze flicked to her rear-view mirror. Her eyes caught a blur of movement. Something red. She took her foot off the accelerator. She didn't know why. It was probably nothing. She searched the mirror again. Nothing. It was gone. But the same feeling of unease she'd had since last night was gnawing at her gut. The car had slowed right down and acting purely on instinct she pulled over and performed a quick U-turn.

She drove back slowly towards where she had seen the flicker of red. Her green eyes searched the side of the road. Nothing but red dirt and brown bush greeted her. She'd almost given up when she saw him. A figure lying just off the edge of the road.

'Hell!' She braked and sprang out of the car, giving the highway only a cursory glance as she crossed it to get to him.

James could see a woman's legs as she strode towards him. She was in long baggy navy shorts that fell to just above her well-defined knees. They were nice legs. Tanned. Smooth. In fact, they were the best damn set of legs he'd ever seen. He'd never been so happy to see a set of legs ever in his life.

If he hadn't been in so much pain he would have laughed. James Remington, gypsy loner, who prided himself on being beholden to no one, was so grateful to this set of legs he'd have traded his bike for them. He shut his eyes and rubbed his St Christopher medallion thankfully.

Helen threw herself down in the dirt beside him. Was this her locum? He looked younger than she'd expected. 'Are you OK?' she demanded, clutching at his jacket.

James opened his eyes and found himself staring into her worried green gaze. Her eyes looked like cool chips of jade. Amber flecks added a touch of heat. It was the only time a demanding woman hadn't scared the hell out of him. In fact, had he not been practically incapacitated with pain, he would have kissed her.

'I am now.' He struggled to sit up.

'No, don't move,' Helen said, pushing him back against the ground. 'Are you James Remington?' she asked as she ran her hands methodically over his body, searching for injuries. Her hands moved dispassionately through his thick wavy hair, feeling for any irregularities or head injuries. Down his neck. Along his collar bones to his shoulders.

He wasn't surprised that she knew who he was. Maybe he should have been but the pain was all-encompassing. As her hands moved lower to feel his chest, push around his rib cage and palpate his abdomen he absently realised he would normally have cracked a joke by now. The pain was obviously altering his persona.

He was pretty suave with the ladies but he'd never had one become so intimately acquainted with his body so quickly. She had a nice face and a distracting prim ponytail that swished from side to side as she assessed his injuries.

'Yes, I am,' he said as her hands gripped his hip bones and she applied pressure down through them, glancing at him with a cocked eyebrow in a silent query. He shook his head.

'We've been worried about you,' she said. 'What happened?' Helen felt methodically down his left leg from groin to toes.

As her fingers brushed his inner thigh James felt his body react despite the pain in his other leg. 'Came off my bike. Cows on the road.' He grimaced.

'Ah. Elsie's,' she said absently as she concentrated on

his other leg, starting again in his right groin. 'You been out here all night?'

'Yup. Look, I'm fine,' James said, batting her hand away. 'It's just my right leg. The tibia's broken.'

Helen sat back on her haunches and surveyed the crude but effective splint. She didn't want to disturb it if she didn't have to. 'Is it closed or open?'

'Closed,' he confirmed. He'd cut open his jeans to investigate the damage by torchlight last night.

'Were you knocked out?'

'No. Conscious the whole time.'

She nodded, grateful to discover that he didn't appear to be too injured at all and trying not to dwell on the fact that their desperately needed locum was now totally useless to them. Helen made a mental note to get onto the agency as soon as she could to organise a replacement.

'Well, we'd better get you to Skye. Do you think between us we can manage to get you into my car? It'll be quicker than calling the ambulance.'

James ran assessing eyes over her. He doubted she'd be much help at all, there wasn't much to her. But he was strong and at the moment he'd go with any option that got him to medical attention as fast as possible. 'Sure.'

Helen nodded and left him to bring her car closer. She performed another U-turn and pulled it up as close to James as possible. She opened the back door.

'You might as well lie along the back seat.'

Helen hoped she'd sounded more confident than she felt. Looking down at him, she wondered how they were going to manage it. There was a lot of him. He was a tall, beefy guy, his build evident despite his recumbent posture.

She remembered the things she had resolutely ignored during her assessment of him. The bulk of his chest, the span of his biceps and the thickness of his quads beneath her hands. He was all man. Still, his musculature had hinted that he took good care of himself. She hoped so. She hoped he was strong enough to lift his bulk because at a petite five two he dwarfed her.

James looked behind him and shuffled his bottom until he was lined up with the open door. 'I can lift myself in if you can support my leg.'

Helen nodded. She knelt to position her hands beneath his splint. She felt him tense and glanced up at him. She noticed the blueness of his eyes for the first time. They were breathtaking. A magnificent turquoise fringed by long sooty lashes. Was it fair for a man to have such beautiful eyes?

She blinked. 'Does it hurt?'

He nodded.

Even through his overnight growth of stubble she noticed the tautness around his mouth and realised what it was costing him to sit stoically.

'It's going to hurt more,' she said softly, knowing there was no way they could accomplish the next manoeuvres without causing more pain.

He nodded again. 'I know.'

'We could wait for Tom. He carries morphine in the ambulance.'

He shook his head and she watched as his thick wavy hair with its occasional grey streaks bounced with the movement and fell across his forehead.

'No. Let's just get it over with.'

She nodded. 'Ready?'

James placed his hands on the car behind him, bent his left leg again and pushed down through his triceps, lifting his bottom off the ground. A pain tore through his fracture site and he grunted and screwed up his face as he placed his rear in the footwell. He shut his eyes and bit his tongue to stop from groaning out loud at the agony seizing his leg.

'You OK?' Helen asked, supporting his leg gently as she noted the sweat beading his brow and his laboured breathing.

James nodded. He felt nausea wash through his system as the pain gnawed away unabated. He had to keep going. If he stopped now he'd never get himself in the car and the pain would kill him. He placed one hand up on the seat and repeated the movement again, lifting his buttocks onto the padded material.

James muttered an expletive and then looked at Helen with apologetic eyes. 'Sorry,' he panted.

Helen grinned. 'Quite all right. I think a swear word is entirely appropriate, given the circumstances.'

'Hardly appropriate in front of a lady.' He grimaced.

Helen looked around her and threw a glance over her shoulder before turning back to face him. 'No ladies here.'

He gave a hearty chuckle and then broke off as pain lanced through his leg and he clutched at the splint. 'Don't make me laugh,' he groaned.

'Whatever the doctor orders.' She grinned.

She held his leg while he shuffled back in the seat and helped him manoeuvre into a position of comfort. Well, of less pain anyway. He dwarfed the back seat. It was impossible for him to recline. Instead, he sat in a semi-supported position, the door propping him up.

'I have some cushions in the boot. Hang tight.'

James closed his eyes wearily feeling grittiness rub like sandpaper against his lids. *Where the hell was he going to go?*

Helen arranged two cushions around his fractured leg to try and support it better. She shut the door and moved around to the driver's side, opening her door and flipping her seat out of the way.

'Here, put this behind your shoulders. Might make the ride a little more comfortable.'

She levered him forwards and stuffed the cushion behind his back, fussing a little to get it just right. James caught a whiff of her perfume and opened his eyes. They were level with her chest and he could see the pink lace of her bra and the curve of her breast as she leaned over him to adjust the cushion.

He shut his eyes again in case she thought he was staring at her breasts, and her ponytail brushed lightly against his face. Her hair was nut brown and smelled like roses. It swished back and forth a few times, caressing his face, and after a night in the cold, dark bush it was strangely comforting. He wanted to wrap it around his fist and pull her closer.

'All set?' she asked.

James slowly opened his eyes. He nodded and smiled. She turned to go and he put a stilling hand on her shoulder. 'Thank you. I don't even know your name.'

'It's Helen. Helen Franklin.'

'Ah. The nurse. That explains your tender touch.'

Helen stilled, suddenly mesmerised by his blue eyes. He was without a doubt the best-looking man she'd ever met. She'd not risked such thinking until now, but it was the inescapable truth.

'Yeah, well, don't count your chickens,' she quipped, pulling away from his touch and resetting her seat. 'We've got a few kilometres of potholed highway to travel first. I'm sure by the end of that you'll have changed your mind.'

Helen buckled up and started the car.

'Be gentle with me, Helen.'

Her eyes flew to the rear-view mirror and found his blue flirty gaze staring back at her. He was teasing her. *Great. Not only sexy but flirty, too.* Fortunately, she knew the type well. Her own father was a classic example. It was typical that not even a broken leg could stymie the natural urge men like James felt to flirt.

But there was a shadow in his eyes that she recognised, too. Something that haunted him. Maybe it was just the pain. But maybe, like her father, it was something deeper, older. Something that he'd carried around for many years. Something that made him wary. Something that made him guarded.

Something that made him…intriguing.

Something that was a big flashing neon sign to her and all women to stay the hell away. Charming and charismatic had their good points but there was always a down side. She'd seen enough to know that men like James Remington, like her father, wouldn't be held back or held still.

She rolled her eyes at him. 'Hang tight.'

She let the tyres spin a few times as she skidded away.

* * *

They made it to the hospital ten minutes later and within half an hour James had been X-rayed and given a shot of morphine.

Helen checked her watch. If she didn't go now she was going to be late for work. They were already one doctor down, necessitating the need for Genevieve to take a patient load when she was supposed to only be working two half-days to show James the ropes before commencing her maternity leave.

Helen worried about Skye's only general practice and what they were going to do without a replacement for Genevieve as she gently drew back the curtain that had been pulled around his cubicle. James lay on the gurney, his eyes shut, his size taking up its entire length, his feet hanging over the end.

He was shirtless and her mouth dried as her gaze skimmed over the planes and angles of his smooth, tanned chest and abdomen. A silver chain hung around his neck, a dainty medallion hanging from it. It looked surprisingly manly and strangely erotic sitting against his broad bare flesh and her fingers itched to touch it.

A light smattering of hair around his flat nipples was tantalising and she followed a trail of hair that arrowed down from his belly button until the sheet cut the rest from her view.

He shifted a little and she looked away from his abdomen, feeling a jolt of guilt at such voyeurism. He smiled to himself and Helen watched as a dimple in his chin transformed his stubbled features from Greek God-like to pure wicked. He looked relaxed for the first time since she'd met him, no tense lines around his mouth or frown marring the gap between his eyebrows.

James was drifting through space, floating. It felt good and he almost sighed as pink lace and roses flitted through the fog in his head. He felt the swish of her hair against his face again, across his lips, and it was as if she'd stroked her hand down his stomach. He could feel himself reaching for her, hear himself murmur her name.

He jolted awake and grabbed the side rails of the gurney as the sensation of falling played tricks with his equilibrium. His foggy mind took a moment to focus and when it did he found himself staring across into green eyes.

'Morphine dreaming?' She smiled.

James had never had anything stronger than paracetamol in his life before so he supposed that was exactly what he'd been doing. 'Strong stuff.' He grimaced.

The floating sensation had been pleasant and the relief from the constant feeling that his leg was in a vice was most welcome, but the sense of not being fully in control of his body was disconcerting and he wasn't entirely sure he liked it. He was always in control. He'd spent too many childhood years feeling helpless to be remotely comfortable with this drug-induced vulnerability.

'I hear you copped a lucky break.'

James grinned at her joke despite the odd feeling of being outside his body. 'Yes, simple fracture of the tibia, not displaced. Long leg cast for six weeks.'

'You got off very easy.'

'Indeed.' James remembered the worst-case scenarios that had careened through his mind as he had been hurled into the bush and knew that he could just as easily be dead or very seriously injured. 'How's my bike?'

She rolled her eyes. Of course, he would be worrying about the machine. 'Alf's recovering it now.'

'You don't approve?'

She shrugged. She was a nurse. Orthopaedic wards were full of motorbike victims. 'Mighty thin doors. No seat belts.'

He regarded her seriously, her no-nonsense ponytail swishing slightly as she spoke. Not a single hair had managed to escape. He grinned. 'You need to live a little. Nothing like the wind on your face, whipping through your hair.'

Helen sucked in a quick breath as his smile made his impossibly handsome face even more so. It made him look every inch the freedom-loving highway gypsy he so obviously was. She understood the pull of the wind in your face—she'd often ridden on the back of her father's bike over the years. But a life of chronic instability had left her with feet firmly planted on the ground.

'I have to get to work. I'll check back in on my lunch-break. Can I bring you anything?'

James shut his eyes as the room started to spin again. 'Food. I'm starving.'

She laughed. 'They do feed you here, you know.'

'Hospital food,' he groaned. 'I want proper stuff.'

'Like?'

James thought hard as the foggy feeling started to take control again. He allowed it to dictate his stomach's needs. He rubbed his hand absently over his hungry belly. 'Pie. Chips with gravy. And a beer.'

Helen laughed again and tried not to be distracted by the slipping of the sheet as his hand absently stroked his stomach. Pies were her favourite bakery item. 'A pie and chips I can do. Don't think morphine and beer are a good mix, though.'

James opened one eye. 'Sister Helen Franklin, you are a spoilsport.'

'Yeah, well, I also sign your cheques so be nice.'

He chuckled and, despite his efforts to fight it, a wave of fog drifted him back into the floating abyss. Being nice to Helen conjured up some very delectable images and with his last skerrick of good sense he hoped it was just the morphine. The feel of her hair in his face and her pink lace was already too interesting fodder for his narcotic-induced fantasies.

If he wasn't careful she might become way more fascinating than was good for him. Helen Franklin looked like she was the kind of woman men stayed with. And James didn't stay. He didn't know how.

CHAPTER TWO

AT SIX o'clock Helen walked into the hospital to find James entertaining three nurses. It had been a shocker of a day. From Elsie and her cows, to finding James, to the news that another locum would be difficult to find. She wasn't feeling particularly jovial.

'Feeling better, I see,' she said dryly.

Her colleagues greeted her warmly and then fluttered their hands at James, promising to catch him later. She frowned at the very married nurses and felt strangely irritated.

'Thank God you're here. Break me out, will you?'

He was sitting propped up in his bed, a black T-shirt thankfully covering his chest, his leg supported on a pillow. She shook her head. Did he think he could just snap his fingers and she'd jump to attention? 'The med super wants to keep you overnight.'

James snorted. 'Don't be ridiculous. I broke my leg, that's all.'

'Jonathon's just being cautious.'

'I'm going stir crazy in here and this bed is frankly the worst thing I've ever lain on. The ground in the bush last night was softer than this.'

Helen laughed despite her irritation because it was true. The mattresses left a lot to be desired. 'How's the cast?' she asked, moving to the end of the bed. 'Wriggle your toes.'

James sighed and wriggled his toes for the hundredth time since he'd had the damn thing put on that morning.

Helen touched them lightly to assess their colour and warmth. 'Do they—?'

'No,' he interrupted. 'They don't tingle. I don't have pins and needles,' he said testily. 'They have perfectly normal sensation.'

Helen quirked an eyebrow. Good, now he was irritated, too. 'So this is the doctors-make-the-worst-patients demonstration?'

'I'd like a decent night's sleep in a comfortable bed before starting work in the morning if it's all the same to you.'

Helen's hand stilled on his toes. 'Work?'

'Yes, work. You know, the reason why I'm in Skye in the first place?'

Helen became aware of her heart beating. She hardly dared to hope. 'Oh…you still want to…take up the contract, then?'

James frowned. 'Of course? Why? Are you withdrawing the offer?'

'No, no, of course not,' she said, absently stroking his toes peeking out from the end of the cast. 'I just assumed… I mean I thought…you'd want to rest up until your leg was out of the cast.'

He snorted and tried not to be distracted by the light touch of her fingers on his toes and how strangely intimate it was. 'It's just a broken leg. I may not be as mobile as I'd like but I'm still capable of sitting in a chair and seeing patients. You do still require a doctor, don't you?'

Helen couldn't believe her luck. Her dark mood lightened. She smiled. 'We most certainly do.'

'Excellent. I'm your guy. Now,' James said as he swung his leg down off the bed and reached for his crutches, 'if you know where my luggage is, perhaps you could get me some clothes and the appropriate paperwork so I can get the hell out of here. I'd like to check on my bike.'.

Helen watched him fit the crutches into his armpits, her hand now lying on the empty pillow.

'It's fine. I went and checked. Alf has it at the garage. He's shut now. You can go visit tomorrow.'

'It'll be safe there?'

She smiled. 'Of course. This is Skye.' Although she did understand his reticence, his classic Harley must be worth a fortune.

He nodded. 'I'll call in on my lunch-hour tomorrow.'

'There's no need to start straight away,' she protested. They could cope for a bit. 'You should take a few days off, James, we'll manage. Your leg should be elevated as much as possible initially.'

'I'll keep it up all night. I promise.'

He turned on the crutches to face her and she tried not to think about the unintended double meaning behind his words. But he was dressed only in his black T-shirt and a pair of black cotton boxer shorts that came to mid-thigh and left nothing to the imagination.

He looked like he could have modelled for them. He would have been perfect in a glossy magazine somewhere with his full pouting mouth and brooding dark looks. She could almost picture him clad only in his undies, his magnificent turquoise eyes making love to the camera. Maybe even straddling a gleaming chrome Harley. James Remington had clearly missed his calling.

She blinked and then swallowed. Hard. For goodness' sake, she was a nurse, not some swooning teenager. She'd seen plenty of completely naked men. It made no sense to be affected by someone who was practically fully clothed. Hell, she'd seen more male skin exposed on a beach.

'Right, then, I'll bring you some clothes. Hang tight.' And she fled from the room.

'Hang tight' seemed to be a favoured expression of hers. Again, as he looked down at his attire, he wondered just where the hell she imagined he would go in his underwear.

James was surprised to find on the way home that he would be living with the very capable Helen Franklin for the duration of his time in Skye. The agency had assured him accommodation was provided so the details hadn't mattered at the time. For someone who'd spent a good part of his life between jobs camped out in a swag on the ground, any roof over his head was welcome.

But as she helped him out of the car and the smell of roses enveloped him again he felt a tug in his groin. The memory of her light touch on his toes earlier returned to him, as did the look she'd given him when he'd stood before her. The amber flecks in her eyes had glowed with warmth, hinting at passion, but she'd also looked a bit like a rabbit caught in headlights.

He could tell she was attracted to him. But he could also tell she didn't want to be. A fact he understood perfectly. He was most definitely attracted to her. Who could resist being plucked out of the bush by pink lace and ponytails? But, like her, he didn't want to be either.

He'd had his share of casual flings on his travels but always with women who'd known the score. Helen Franklin sent up a big red flag in his head. Warning bells were ringing loudly. Some women were best left alone— and she was one of them.

'So this is it,' Helen said, dumping her bag on the hall-stand and holding the door open for him. He brushed past her on the crutches and her breath hitched in her throat. 'Your bags are in your room, through there.'

Helen pointed to one of the three bedrooms that ran off the main living area and tried not to blush at the memory of going through his bags to find the clothes he was now wearing. There had been a lot of boxers in his luggage and she felt as if she knew him more intimately than she'd ever known a complete stranger.

'Kitchen through that door and dining room beside it.' Helen could feel his gaze on her. 'I have a casserole from last night I plan on heating up, if you'd like some.'

James nodded, his stomach growling at the suggestion. 'Sounds good. I wouldn't mind a shower first, though. I feel like half the bush is still clinging to me.' He looked down at his leg and grimaced. 'I guess a bath's going to be easier.'

Helen nodded while desperately trying to not think about him in the bath. Naked. 'Probably.' *Oh, God, he wasn't going to need a hand, was he?* 'Will you be OK to…?'

James watched the play of emotions flick across her face and toyed with the idea of exaggerating his injury. 'Why? Are you offering?' he murmured.

Helen felt her cheeks grow hot just thinking about something that was second nature to her. Something that she had helped hundreds of patients with. Running a bath for him…helping him off with his clothes…supporting him as he lowered himself into the bath. She opened her mouth to tell him she wasn't his nursemaid but no words come out.

James chuckled. 'It's OK, Helen. I think you've already gone above and beyond the call of duty.'

She cleared her throat and tried again. 'Damn right,' she said, and stalked into the kitchen, his hearty laughter following her.

An hour later Helen was starting to worry when the door to the bathroom was still closed. She hadn't heard any pleas for help and she hoped he was just taking his time rather than stuck in the bath, unable to get out. She turned the volume on the television up to distract her from her steamy thoughts.

He joined her a few minutes later, hobbling on his crutches. He was wearing a white T-shirt that hugged his well-defined musculature and a pair of black boxer shorts. His dark wavy hair was damp and wet strings of it brushed the back of his neck. He smelled like soap and something else, some spicy fragrance that she knew was going to stick around long after he'd hit the road.

He was clean shaven and her fingers tingled with the urge to touch his smooth jaw.

'Better?' she asked him, hoping she sounded normal and that the husky strain in her voice was just her imagination. She'd known him for less than a day but already he made her acutely aware that she was a woman.

He nodded. 'Heaps.'

James turned to sit on a lounge chair.

'No, wait, hang on,' she said, springing up from the couch she'd been sitting on. 'You have the three-seater— that way you can put your leg up. I'll sit there.'

James stopped and stared down at her. She was fussing around with cushions. She seemed nervous. Her ponytail swished with her movements and from his vantage point he could see the nip of her waist and the nape of her neck.

'OK.' He sat and put his leg up gratefully. It had started to throb again and he'd just taken two painkillers.

'Hang tight. I'll just nuke your casserole.'

Helen fled to the kitchen and leant heavily against the sink for a moment. *What the hell was happening to her?* She was acting as if she'd never seen a man before. OK, they didn't really get men of his calibre in Skye. For God's sake, there were only three unattached men under forty and not one of them looked like James. Locums who deigned to come to the bush usually only came in one flavour— fiftyish, balding and, more often than not, condescending.

But she was going to need to get a serious grip because she had to live with this man for four months and acting like a tongue-tied teenager every time she saw him less than fully dressed was going to get really embarrassing really quickly. So he redefined tall, dark and handsome. One thing was for sure. He'd get back on that bike in four months' time and ride off into the sunset. And she was damned if he was going to ride off with her heart.

James looked up as she came back into the room carrying a steaming bowl of something that smelled divine, and his stomach growled. He took the tray from her and was pleased to see she'd served him a hearty portion and also added a hunk of fresh grainy bread.

'This smells amazing,' he said as he ripped off a chunk of bread and dipped it into the thick, dark gravy.

Helen nodded. 'It tastes pretty good, too.'

James mouth was salivating even before he could put the soaked bread into it. He shut his eyes and sighed as the meaty flavour hit his taste buds. He chewed and savoured it for a few moments before swallowing. 'Oh, yes. Yes, it does.'

Helen resolutely turned her attention to the television and tried not to be turned on by the sounds of pleasure coming from his direction. Elsie had always said there was nothing more satisfying than filling a grown man's belly. Helen had secretly thought that was kind of old-fashioned but being privy to James's appreciation was strangely gratifying.

As James ate he watched his new housemate surreptitiously through his heavy fringe. She seemed engrossed in the television, sitting with her shapely legs crossed and her hands folded primly in her lap. She was quite petite and the big squishy leather chair seemed to envelop her.

She was still in her clothes from that morning, navy shorts which had ridden up to mid-thigh and a plain white cotton blouse. He assumed it was her uniform. Apart from the tantalising glimpse of her leg, it was kind of shapeless. If he hadn't known about the pink lace beneath he would have even said it was boring.

'So, what's the story with this place?' James asked as he mopped up the dregs of his bowl with the last piece of bread. 'It looks quite old.'

Helen steeled herself to look at him and was grateful he was looking at the fancy ceiling cornices. 'It's a turn-of-the-century worker's cottage that's been added onto over the years. It's been used as a residence for the Skye Medical Practice for about forty years since Dr Jones bought the property and built the original surgery at the front of the land.'

'Did he live in it?'

Helen nodded. 'Until it got too small for his growing family. He had seven children. And it's been used ever since by successive doctors. Frank lived in it when he first came to Skye until they bought something bigger, so did Genevieve until she moved in with Don.'

'Frank's the boss?'

Helen nodded.

'Has it ever been empty?'

'Off and on.'

'How long have you lived here?'

Since Duncan and Denise's growing brood had made her realise it had been time to move on. They hadn't asked her to go, had been horrified when she had suggested it, but she'd known it was the right thing to do. As welcome as they'd always made her, as much a part of the family as she'd always been, the facts were the facts. They'd needed an extra room and she was an adult.

It had been an odd time. She'd realised that she'd never had a place she could truly call her own. A place she'd felt like she'd belonged. That deep down, despite Elsie's love and assurances, she'd always felt on the outside. Her mother was gone and her father was more comfortable with the open road than his own daughter.

She looked around, feeling suddenly depressed. Even this place wasn't hers. 'A couple of years.'

James heard a sadness shadowing her answer. He saw it reflected in her eyes. He recognised the look. Had seen it in his own eyes often enough. Beneath the surface Helen Franklin was as solitary as him. Looking for something to make her feel whole. Just like him.

He felt a strange connection to her and had a sudden urge to pull her close, and perhaps if he hadn't been encumbered with a cast that seemed to weigh a ton he might have. She seemed so fragile suddenly, so different from the woman who had dragged him from the bush. 'Is that how long you've lived in Skye?'

Helen laughed. 'Goodness, no. I was born here.'

Of course. Everything about her screamed homey. From her casserole to her prim ponytail. She looked utterly at home in this cosy worker's cottage in outback Queensland.

He felt a growl hum through his bloodstream as the affinity he'd felt dissolved with a rush of hormones. She wasn't his type. In fact, she was the type he avoided like the plague.

'Have you lived here all your life?'

Helen didn't miss the slight emphasis on the word 'all'. Obviously staying in one place was a fate worse than death for him. She looked at his beautiful face, into his turquoise gaze, and saw the restlessness there. The same restlessness she'd grown up seeing in her father's eyes. He was a drifter. A gypsy.

'Except for when I went to uni.'

James nodded his head absently. *Definitely not his type.* He preferred women who had lived life a bit. Travelled. In his experience they were much more open-minded. They knew the score and didn't expect an engagement ring the second a man paid them a bit of attention.

'You don't approve.'

He shrugged. 'Not at all. It's just not for me. I'd feel too hemmed in.'

Heed his words, Helen, heed his words. But a part of her rebelled. The arrogance of the man to assume that because she was still living in the place she'd been born that she'd not done anything with her life. 'There's nothing wrong with being grounded. Doesn't running away get tiresome?'

He chuckled at her candour. She didn't look fragile any more. She looked angry. 'I prefer to think of it as moving on.'

God, he sounded like her father. 'I bet you do.' He chuckled again and goose-bumps feathered her arm as if he'd stroked his finger down it. 'So where are you *moving on* to from here?'

He shrugged. 'Central Queensland somewhere. Wherever they need a locum. I haven't seen much of the state and I want to make my way up to the Cape. It's supposed to be spectacular.'

Helen had been up to Cape York with her father during a very memorable school holiday. It *was* spectacular. But stubbornness prevented her from sharing that thought. She wasn't going to elaborate and spoil his image of her as a small-town, gone-nowhere girl.

'Where are you from originally?'

'Melbourne. But I haven't lived there since I finished my studies.'

'Let me guess. You've been travelling?'

James laughed. 'Very good.'

'Do you still have family in Melbourne?'

'My mother.'

Helen noticed the way his smile slipped a little. It didn't appear that they were close. 'Your father?'

James sobered as he fingered the chain around his neck. 'He died in my final year of uni.'

'I'm sorry,' Helen said quietly. She met his turquoise gaze and she could see regret and sorrow mingle.

He shrugged. 'We weren't really close.'

There were a few moments when neither of them spoke. The television murmuring in the background was the only noise. So James's relationship with his parents had been as fraught as hers had been with her parents? She felt a moment of solidarity with him.

James stirred before the sympathy he saw in her gaze blindsided him to the facts. Helen Franklin was a woman who liked to be grounded. He'd avoided her type for years.

They were incompatible. He was just a little weakened from the pain that was starting to gnaw at his leg again and her terrific home cooking.

'Still, I inherited his bike. I guess I have that to thank him for.'

That explained why he'd been so concerned about the

machine. It wasn't just because it was highly valuable, it obviously had sentimental value to him.

'She's a beautiful Harley,' Helen commented. 'Is it a '60 or '61?'

James regarded her for a moment. 'You know something about bikes?'

Helen stifled the smile that sprang to her lips at his amazement. 'I know a little.'

'It's a 1960.'

'It seemed to survive the crash OK.'

He smiled. 'An oldy but a goody.'

She grinned back at him. It was something her father would have said, his own classic Harley being his most prized possession. Looking at James, she could see why her mother had fallen for her father. The whole free-spirit thing was hard to resist. James's handsome face was just as charming, just as charismatic as the man who had fathered her.

She blinked. 'So…what…you just roam around the country, going from one locum job to the next?'

He nodded. 'Pretty much.'

'Sounds…interesting.' Actually, she thought it sounded terrible. No continuity. No getting to know your patients or your colleagues or your neighbours. It sounded lonely.

'Oh, it is. I love it. The bush is drastically underserviced. There are so many practices crying out for locums. Too many GPs working themselves into the ground because they can't take any time off. Much more than city practices. I really feel like I fill a need out here. And bush people are always so friendly and happy to see you.'

'But don't you ever long to stay in one place for a while? Really get to know people?'

He shrugged. 'I prefer to spread myself around. Locums are in such high demand out here—'

'Tell me about it,' Helen interrupted.

He smiled. 'I'd like to think I can help as many stressed out country GPs as I can rather than just a few for longer. And, anyway, it suits my itchy feet.'

She suspected James Remington could have done anything he'd put his mind to. He looked like a hot-shot surgeon at home breaking hearts all over a big city hospital yet he chose to lose himself in the outback. 'Not a lot of money in it,' she commented.

'I do all right,' he said dismissively. 'General practice has its own rewards.'

As an only child growing up in a very unhappy household, James had never felt particularly wanted by either of his parents. Oh, he hadn't been neglected or abused but he'd been left with the overwhelming feeling of being in the way. Being in the way of their happiness. They'd stayed together for him and had been miserable.

Being a GP, especially in the country, looking after every aspect of a patient's health, had made him feel more wanted and needed than his parents ever had. Not just by his patients but by his colleagues and the different communities he'd serviced. And James knew through painful experience you couldn't put a dollar value on that. Some rewards were greater than any riches.

Helen nodded. 'I agree.'

They watched television for a while. Helen found her gaze drifting his way too frequently for her own liking. She yawned. 'Think I'm going to turn in for the night.' She stood and leaned over to take his tray, his spicy scent luring her closer.

'Yes, I'm kind of done in myself.'

She straightened, pulling herself away. 'See you in the morning.'

'Night,' he called after her retreating back.

James woke at two a.m. his leg throbbing relentlessly. He shifted around trying to get comfortable for fifteen minutes and gave up when no amount of position change eased the constant gnaw. He reached for his crutches and levered himself out of bed. He'd left his painkillers in the bathroom.

Quietly he navigated his way through the unfamiliar house to the bathroom. He didn't want to switch on any lights in case he woke Helen. He didn't know whether she was a light sleeper or not and the last thing he wanted to do was annoy her on their first night under the same roof.

He located the pills and swallowed two, washing them down with some tap water. The thought of trying to get back to sleep before the painkillers had worked their magic didn't appeal so James decided to sit in the lounge, put the television on low and try and distract himself.

He picked his way gingerly through the lounge room, trying not to make too much noise or bang into any furniture. He felt for the couch as he balanced himself on his crutches and was grateful when he finally found the edge. But as he manoeuvred down into its squishy folds his crutches wobbled and one of them fell.

James made a grab for it but the sudden movement

jarred through his fracture site. He cursed to himself as he clutched his leg, helpless to prevent the crutch from crashing down loudly on the coffee-table.

Helen sprang from her bed as the noise pulled her out of her sleep. James? Had he fallen? She dashed outside pushing her sleep-mussed hair out of her face.

She snapped on the light, flooding the lounge room in a fluorescent glow, putting her hand to her eyes at the sudden pain stabbing into her eyeballs. 'What? What's wrong?'

James squinted, too, the pain in his leg still gripping unbearably.

'Are you OK?' Helen asked, slowly removing her hand as her eyes adjusted.

He nodded. 'Sorry, I didn't mean to wake you.'

James's eyes came open slowly and he wondered if the pain and the medication were making him delirious. Before him stood a very different Helen Franklin. Gone was the prim ponytail. Her hair was down, a deep rich brown tumbling in sleep-mussed disorder to her shoulders. It made him want to put his face into it, glide his fingers through it.

Gone was the shapeless uniform. She was wearing some kind of silky sleep shirt the colour of a fine merlot, which barely skimmed the tops of her thighs and clung in interesting places. It left him in no doubt that her pert breasts were no longer encased in pink lace. In any lace at all. He could see the jut of her hip and the curve of her waist and a whole lot of leg.

A sudden image of her riding on the back of his Harley

dressed as she was right now, her breasts pushed against his back, stormed his mind and he was rendered temporarily mute. That medication he'd been given was powerful stuff!

'Oh, no!'

James roused himself at her plaintive cry and tracked her progress with eyes that seemed to be seeing in slow motion only. Her body moved interestingly beneath her silk shirt.

She was kneeling beside the coffee-table, gathering some broken glass from a photo frame, before he registered what had happened.

'Oh, hell. Sorry. I didn't realise I'd broken anything. I'll replace it.'

Helen looked down at the broken glass that had framed a picture of her at fifteen and her father on his Harley. 'It's OK,' she said dismissively, tracing his devil-may-care smile. 'It's just glass. I can replace it. I should remove my pictures anyway. I've been here by myself for so long I kind of took over.'

'No, please, don't.' He placed a hand on hers. 'I'm only here temporarily, it would be silly to put them away.'

Helen looked down at his big hand covering hers. *Only temporary.* Just like the guy in the photo.

James removed his hand and watched the way she touched the picture with a strange kind of loving reverence. 'Your dad?'

Helen nodded, still staring down at the photo.

'Is he…?'

She glanced up at him as he trailed off. His hair was sleep-tousled, his wavy fringe flopping across his forehead, and she was pleased that the coffee-table was between them. 'No. He's very much alive and roaming some highway somewhere.'

He saw the love in her eyes as she gazed at the picture but heard the bitter note in her voice. Obviously her father aroused intense emotions. It also explained how she knew about Harleys. And maybe it even explained her desire to stay grounded.

'Anyway,' she said, becoming aware of his intense gaze and the building silence and belatedly the fact that she was in her pajamas, 'are you going to be OK?'

He nodded. 'I'm just going to watch some telly until the painkillers start to take effect.'

Helen rose and backed away, still clutching the frame. She was suddenly acutely aware of her state of undress. How bare her thighs were. How braless she was. How her shirt barely covered her rear. How…interested he seemed.

'See you in the morning.' She took a deep breath and turned at the last moment, praying that he wasn't watching her.

But he was. James caught a brief glimpse of firm cheek as the shirt flared when she whipped around. And leg. A lot of leg. Suddenly his time in Skye had become very interesting indeed.

He was living with someone who was as sexy as hell underneath her ponytailed primness and knew about Harleys.

Suddenly she seemed more and more his type.

CHAPTER THREE

HELEN didn't dare come out into the main part of the house until she was dressed the next morning. She'd lain awake for an hour, thinking about James's heated gaze and how liquid heat had pooled low in her belly. She knew that even after a day in his company she was treading on dangerous ground.

She was attracted to him. Not such a bad thing to admit to, she supposed, except for the fact that he was way out of her league. The regular attentions of Skye's bachelors paled into comparison with one hot look from James. She'd do well to remember he was only there for four months and she'd never had a casual relationship in her life.

When she was dressed she made her way out to the lounge room to find James fast asleep where she'd left him. She stopped in mid-stride and almost tripped. The man was utterly gorgeous. A dark shadow adorned his jaw and his broad chest rose and fell in hypnotic splendour. His jet-black hair lay thick and luscious across his forehead.

His leg was raised on some cushions. His other leg

positively exuded testosterone, its well-defined quadri-
ceps and calf muscles complemented by a perfect covering
of dark hair. His large bare foot seemed oddly out of place
with his sexy he-man image, made him seem vulnerable
somehow, and the nurturer in her wanted to go get a
blanket and cover him up.

She gave herself a mental shake and ordered herself to
stop gawking like a teenager. She turned away and headed
for the kitchen. Damn him for lying around her house,
looking sexy and vulnerable all at once. She got two slices
of bread and jammed them into the toaster. She pushed the
lever down harder than required and hoped he had almighty
backache this morning. If she had to trip over his barely
covered body every morning, it was going to be a long four
months!

James awoke slowly. He could hear music and noises
coming from the kitchen and the mouth-watering aroma
of toast teased his nostrils. He grimaced as he sat up and
rubbed the crick in his neck. There was a slight ache in his
leg but it was feeling much better than it had last night
when his midnight wanderings had disturbed Helen.

A vision of her in her sleep shirt played in his mind again
and he smiled to himself. Maybe it had been the medication,
maybe it had been seeing a scantily clad Helen in the middle
of the night, but something had fuelled some fairly erotic
dreams and he felt his loins heat as he recalled the images.

He rose awkwardly, using his crutches for support. He
needed a shower. A cold one. But given how logistically
impossible that would be, he'd settle for coffee instead. He
hoped Helen owned some decent stuff, not some horrible
instant brand.

Even on the road he made sure he carried a supply of freshly ground coffee. Life was too short to drink the instant stuff. In fact, that was pretty much his motto for life. Life was short, grab it by the horns and ride it for all it was worth. He'd grown up seeing his parents waste their lives stuck in a situation they hadn't wanted to be in, and he was damned if he would.

He drank good coffee. He went where he wanted. He followed his own rules. He worked wherever the road took him and kept his relationships short and sweet. And even if his heart did occasionally yearn for something more, he hadn't been in a place yet or met a woman yet who could ground him. In fact, he seriously doubted either existed.

He swung into the kitchen and stopped in the doorway. Helen was standing at the sink, her back to him, eating toast as she bopped along to a country song playing on the radio. Her head was moving to the beat, her hips were swaying and her feet tapping.

He leant heavily on his crutches for support. She was back in her uniform again, her hair tied back in its prim ponytail, not a hair out of place. But it didn't stop the leap of interest in his groin or a pang of something he couldn't quite name hitting him in the chest. He knew she probably had some lacy concoction on under that prim white blouse, knew the contours of her hips from the cling of fabric last night, knew that her bottom cheeks were cute and perky as hell.

She could be the one. James clutched the handles of the crutches harder as the insidious voice invaded his head. Preposterous! Yes, he fancied her. He was a man, for crying out loud, and she was a very attractive woman. But that was it.

For God's sake, he'd only known her for a day. OK, it had been a tumultuous day. She had, after all, rescued him and his broken leg from the bush, but there was no need to let his imagination get carried away.

The funny feeling he'd got in his chest when he'd looked at her just now was easily explained. It was lust. The tantalising stirrings of sexual attraction. The allure of possibility. And that was all. He was a thirty-five-year-old man. *He* was in charge of his life—not his hormones.

He cleared his throat. 'I don't suppose you have any decent coffee in this neck of the woods?'

Helen jumped. She hadn't heard him approach. She turned. 'You nearly gave me a heart attack,' she said accusingly, talking around her last mouthful of toast.

He grinned. 'Sorry. I was enjoying the show, though.'

Helen swallowed the remnants of her breakfast. How long had he been standing there? She straightened and gave him a don't-mess-with-me look. 'Show's over.'

He shrugged. 'I prefer rock music anyway. Does the local radio station play any of that?'

'Sure. Country rock.'

James chuckled. 'About that coffee?'

Helen pointed to the percolator sitting on the bench and the expensive coffee-jar sitting beside it.

James eyes lit up at the unexpected sight of his favourite Italian blend. Helen Franklin may live in outback Queensland but she obviously had style. 'Ah, a woman who appreciates fine coffee.'

Helen shrugged. 'Life's too short to drink bad coffee.'

James gaze caught and held hers as she echoed his sentiment. Living with a gorgeous woman who shared one of life's most basic truths with him was going to be a bigger challenge to his powers of resistance than he'd first thought. 'Couldn't have put it better myself,' he said softly.

Helen swallowed at the silky quality to his words. His magnetic presence made the small kitchen seem even tinier. 'Why don't you go and get dressed?' *For God's sake, put something on...* 'And I'll get a pot started.'

James nodded noticing how she clutched her hands together. 'Deal.' He grinned and executed a perfect about-turn on his crutches.

They walked the short distance to work in a silence broken only by the crunching of their feet on the pebbles that lined the drive. The day was already hot and James turned his face towards the sun.

'Here we are,' Helen said, opening the back door for him and indicating for him to precede her.

James swung in on his crutches into what appeared to be a staffroom and was greeted by a very pregnant freckled redhead.

'Ah, you must be James. Thank God you're here,' Genevieve said, and gave him an enthusiastic hug.

James laughed. It wasn't often that he was greeted like Santa had dropped him under a tree. 'You must be Genevieve.'

'Yes, sorry,' she said, blushing a pretty shade of pink. 'Probably not the most appropriate way of saying hello but you are a sight for sore eyes...or feet, as the case may be.'

Helen envied the easy way Genevieve handled herself around James. She felt all tongue-tied just looking at him—there was no way she could have just casually hugged him. Although Genevieve did have a compelling motive so greeting James like he was a long lost-brother seemed entirely appropriate.

'Well, I aim to please.' James smiled.

Helen heard the flirty tone to his voice and wanted to roll her eyes. Did the man never switch his charm off? Genevieve was happily married and hugely pregnant.

'Genevieve's right,' said a gruff voice from the doorway. 'You are a sight for sore eyes.'

James looked up and saw a big bear of a man with a thick bushy beard standing in the doorway. 'You're not going to hug me are you?' he joked.

The man roared laughing. 'Hardly.' He walked forward, extending his hand. 'Frank. Frank Greer. Nice to have you in Skye, James. Are you sure your leg's up to it?'

'It aches a little still but work will help to keep my mind off it.'

'I hope Helen's been looking after you.'

The image of a silky sleep shirt flared against his retina. He looked at a glowering Helen. 'Yes, she has. She's been great.'

Helen glared at Frank. If her boss thought she was going to play doctors and nurses with James Remington, he could think again. 'In case it has escaped your notice, it is not part of my job to nursemaid every locum that decides to crash his bike and break his leg. Nursemaiding you two is more than enough!' She glared at James for good measure. *Don't get any fancy ideas.*

Frank roared with laughter. 'You're right. What would we do without you? She's marvelous, James, just marvellous.'

Genevieve nodded. 'She runs this practice like clock-work.'

'Damn right I do. Best you both remember that at lunch when I intend to ask for a pay rise.'

They laughed and James could feel the easy affection between the three of them as a palpable force.

'Well I'd love to stand around and chat but I've got work to do. Guess I'll start with the coffee as no one else has done it.'

Helen flicked a reproving glance at her two colleagues. She did love them but would it kill either of them to put the coffee on for once? This was what she got for being indispensable and babying them all these years. She stowed her bag in a cupboard and approached the sink.

'Come on, James, I'll show you the ropes,' Genevieve said, rubbing her belly.

He looked at the mother-to-be and saw the dark circles under her eyes, noted the way she shifted from foot to foot and pushed at her ribs as if she just couldn't get comfortable. She looked exhausted and it wasn't even eight in the morning.

'There's no need,' he said. 'All I need to know is the way to my office. I'll figure the rest out as I go along. I've been a locum for the last five years, I'm used to feeling my way.' True, each practice was slightly different, but the fundamentals never changed.

'But—'

'Really,' James insisted, moving towards her and pulling out a chair from the table behind her. 'Sit, you look done in. It's my fault you had to work a full day yesterday. I think you should just go home and put your feet up. Look after that little one and yourself.'

'I…' Genevieve said as she sank into the chair and looked at Frank.

'It's more than OK by me.' Frank nodded.

James saw the flare of hope and longing in her eyes battle with the weight of her responsibilities. 'Really, I'll be fine. And Helen will be able to tell me what I need to know. Right, Helen?'

Helen turned to face them. Her conscience battled with her libido. She didn't want to spend the morning in such close quarters with him and, damn it, she was busy enough without his professional needs to see to. But one look at Genevieve's weariness and she knew she couldn't deny him. He'd been sensitive enough to Genevieve's obvious exhaustion and it'd be churlish of her to ignore it.

She plastered a smile on her face. 'Sure, absolutely. James is right. Go home. We'll manage just fine.'

'It would be nice to…take a load off,' Genevieve admitted.

'Well, that's sorted, then,' James said, placing a brotherly hand on her arm and easing her up out of the chair. 'Off with you now. We don't want to see you around here until you come to show the little guy off.'

'How do you know it's going to be a boy?' she asked.

Helen handed Genevieve her bag. 'He's a male. They're kind of egocentric like that,' she said dryly.

James's swift laughter took her breath away. It was deep and sexy and one hundred per cent male. The man was impossible to insult! She watched him and Frank usher Genevieve out of the room and contemplated her day. A traitorous thrill ran through her body. If this was day one, how the hell was she ever going to get through the next four months?

* * *

He was right, Helen decided half an hour later. He was a quick study. She'd shown him his office, Frank's office, the reception area, the treatment rooms, the phone system, the chart system and the storeroom. He'd asked a few intelligent questions and clarified several points, but otherwise had listened and not interrupted.

'Here's your appointment book,' she said as she sat in her chair behind the front desk.

James scanned the bookings. 'Doesn't look too intense.'

'You're fairly light today because Genevieve's been taking a reduced patient load. That'll change by week's end.'

'Oh?'

'Once the town finds out you're here, we'll have an influx of patients with all sorts of fictitious conditions, coming to check out the new doctor.'

James laughed. He'd witnessed that phenomenon before. 'I'll try not to disappoint them.'

Helen doubted he'd disappoint at all. The man was going to set off a swooning epidemic all over town.

'So we break at one for lunch?' he asked, studying the book.

Helen nodded. 'One till two.'

'That'll give me time to go to Alf's and check on the bike.'

The bike. 'You're not going to be able to ride it for a while,' she pointed out as she tapped a pencil against his cast.

He grimaced. 'I know. Not quite sure how I'll take that. I'll probably go stir crazy.'

'Trapped in a small town with no way of escape your worst nightmare?'

He shook his head. 'Not at all. I just rarely go a day without riding it. I like the sense of freedom it gives me.'

James's words echoed her father's in her head. Her very lovable, very charismatic, very absent father. Freedom? It seemed to her he was as shackled as the next person. Always out there looking for something he could never quite find. 'Are you free or just lost?'

James looked down into her earnest face, her steady green gaze. How did you explain the call of the road to a homebody? But gazing at her, the frission between them pulsing steadily, he wanted her to understand.

'It's hard to explain.'

They gazed at each other for a few moments, his turquoise stare meeting unwavering green. 'Try me.'

The door opened and the first customer of the day stepped inside. Their eye contact held briefly until the patient spoke and then Helen looked away and smiled at one of Frank's regulars. She felt James's intense gaze for a few more moments and almost sagged against the desk when he hobbled to his office and shut the door.

James sat at his desk and mulled over the strange conversation. How could he explain something that was so innate? And why was it so damn important that she understand? He was out of Skye in four months and whether Helen Franklin got it or not was neither here nor there. She was just another pretty face in just another small town. And out of bounds at that.

His intercom buzzed and her husky voice announcing his first patient pushed past his resolve and made a mockery of his don't-give-a-damn attitude.

'Send them in.'

It was lunchtime before he knew it. He'd seen fifteen patients all with varying conditions who had welcomed him warmly to Skye. His leg ached slightly and he had garnered a lot of sympathy over the course of the morning. He'd even managed to find most things without having to hassle Helen too much.

Yes, he thought as he made his way across the main street to Alf's Garage, he had slipped into the routine of Skye's only general practice easily. It was going to be a very pleasant time here indeed. The Helen factor was something he hadn't counted on but it was nothing he couldn't handle.

It was hot outside. The summer sun high in the sky beat down on him relentlessly and shimmered off the bitumen in a haze as he waited for a couple of cars to pass. He looked up and down the main street with interest.

It was like a hundred other small towns he'd seen throughout rural Australia. Wide and a little potholed, there was a central strip for parking along which jacaranda trees had been planted to provide shade and a dazzling carpet of purple in October.

There were the required four pubs, one on every corner, their beautiful wrought-iron latticework decorating the wide verandahs and tin roofs of the solid two-storey structures. Locals strolled down the streets, taking respite from the heat under the shady shop awnings. A bakery. A butcher. A newsagent. A milk bar. The usual array of bread-and-butter services lining main streets everywhere in outback towns.

James spent ten minutes chatting with Alf and looking over his banged-up bike. Assessing the damage, he was amazed he hadn't been more injured. He gave Alf the number of a classic Harley specialist in Melbourne and left reluctantly.

The bike was more than just something that had been bequeathed to him in his father's will. More than just a connection to a man who'd always considered his son as some sort of cross to bear. The Harley was the bike his father had finally left on after years of a miserable marriage and as such symbolised freedom to James.

Freedom to be happy. Freedom to plot your own course. Freedom from blame. He'd never seen his father happier than the day he'd ridden away, the Harley between his legs.

His stomach grumbled and James decided to cross back over and buy a pie from the bakery. The one Helen had bought him yesterday had been amazing and he'd been craving another ever since. He spotted Helen walking by as he queued and he bought two on impulse.

He exited the shop and looked down the street in the direction Helen had been heading. He saw her in the distance and hurried to catch her up, his crutches a hindrance to speed. She stopped, turned right, opened a gate and disappeared from sight. When he finally drew level he saw it was an old hall. It stood on stumps, a rickety-looking staircase leading to an open door. The sign above the door read SKYE COUNTRY WOMEN'S ASSOCIATION. Helen was in the CWA? Wasn't that for oldies?

He shrugged, opened the gate, swung down the short path and manoeuvred himself up the stairs, following her in. The hall was spacious inside, its bare floorboards and pitched roof causing the low murmur of voices to echo hollowly around the room. A raised stage at the far end was overlooked by a framed picture of the Queen.

About twenty elderly women sat on chairs arranged in a circle. Behind them a trestle table groaned with food. The voices cut off as he entered. The click-clack of dozens of knitting needles ground to a halt.

They looked at him. Helen looked up from her knitting as the silence stretched. Her heart slammed in her chest. *What the hell was he doing here?* Wasn't it bad enough they had to live and work together?

'I bought you a pie,' he said, holding up the brown bakery packet, acutely aware of his very attentive audience.

Helen met his turquoise gaze, refusing to pay her hammering heart any heed. 'Are you following me?'

He smiled. 'Just repaying the favour.'

Elsie looked at Helen and saw the slight flush to her cheeks. She looked back at the stranger. He must be the missing locum Helen had been telling her about yesterday. Fine specimen of a man. 'Do you know how to knit, son?' Elsie asked.

'No, ma'am.' He shook his head. 'My grandmother tried to teach me once.' James smiled at the memory. His mother's mother had always made him feel wanted. 'She said I had two left thumbs.'

The women chuckled. 'Well, never mind, bring that pie over here then and pull up a pew. Helen needs some meat on her bones.'

James gave Helen a doubtful look. He loved the sense of community in small towns and had been in enough to know that the CWA ladies were the queen bees. But he hadn't been in town long enough to get a good sense of everything yet and he didn't want to blow it in front of Skye's matriarchs. 'I don't want to intrude.'

'Nonsense,' Elsie said. 'We never knock back the company of a handsome young man, do we, ladies?'

There was a general murmur of agreement and James smiled. He acquiesced, making his way towards the circle, and the knitting needles started up again.

Helen pulled up a chair for him next to Elsie. 'You're really getting around on those things,' she said testily.

He grinned and passed her the pie. 'I'm getting better.'

She took the packet from him as he settled himself down. 'Lucky for you I have a pie fetish.'

Too much information. The less he knew about her fetishes, the easier the next four months would be.

'So, you're the locum our cows upended in the bush,' Elsie said with a twinkle in her eye.

James chuckled. 'Apparently.'

Helen went around the circle and introduced all the ladies. She watched as each of them, none under seventy, primped and preened at James's effortless flirting. The man was lethal.

She ate the pie, luxuriating in its rich meaty flavour, trying her best to ignore the conversation and the deep rumble of James's voice as he spoke.

'So, what are we working on, ladies? Is this a general knitting circle or is this a specific project?'

'It's for the Royal Children's Hospital in Brisbane,' Elsie said. 'We knit trauma teddies and bootees and bonnets for the little kiddies.'

'That's very admirable,' he commented.

'Keeps us occupied.' Elsie shrugged. 'Tell us a bit about yourself.'

James was used to the questions and gave the ladies a potted history of his time as an outback locum. He regaled them with his travel anecdotes and skilfully sidestepped any questions that got too personal.

'He reminds me of Owen, don't you think, Helen?' Elsie asked.

Helen ignored the general murmur of agreement. 'Not really,' she said briskly.

'Owen?' James asked.

'Helen's father,' Elsie said.

James saw the shuttered look on Helen's face and gave a noncommittal 'Ah.' He knew how closely he guarded his own history. The last thing he wanted was to encourage these chatty women, even though he was curious.

Elsie also got the message loud and clear and changed tack. She was getting old. And Helen was like the grand-daughter she'd never had. Helen had had such a tough life, Elsie would love to see her settled soon. And there was something about this man, about the way Helen was around him, that brought out the matchmaker in her.

'I hope you're looking after my girl, James. I do so worry about her living by herself.'

Helen almost inhaled the tea she'd been drinking. 'Elsie,' she warned, after she'd recovered from a coughing fit. 'I don't need anyone to take care of me.'

'Nonsense,' Elsie said. 'Everyone needs someone. Isn't that right, ladies?' The circle backed Elsie's statement vigorously. 'You should both come over for tea one night. I make a mean lamb roast, isn't that right, Helen?'

Helen shot an apologetic look at James as the other women agreed. She stabbed her knitting needles through the ball of wool. 'We'd better get back,' she said, standing abruptly.

James bit the inside of his cheek. He felt sorry for Helen. He'd been put on the spot so many times by so many elderly ladies at such gatherings he'd come to expect it. But Helen looked totally mortified, comically so.

They were out in the sunshine in under a minute.

'I'm very sorry about Elsie.'

He laughed. 'It's OK. I think it's some unwritten law that once you get past seventy you have to embarrass as many of the younger generation as possible.'

Helen laughed, relieved that he didn't seemed worried by Elsie's attempts to matchmake. 'I think you're right.'

'You and Elsie seem very close.'

She nodded. 'She practically raised me.'

He looked down at her. 'Your parents?'

'My mother was…ill…a lot and my father…well, let's just say my father didn't cope well. I lived out at Elsie's farm on and off for a long time and when my mother died I just…stayed.'

Helen's childhood sounded as bleak as his. 'That's pretty amazing of her.'

'Yes,' she agreed. 'She's a pretty amazing woman.'

They continued on in silence for a little longer, James reflecting on his own barren childhood. 'Do I really look like him? Your father?'

Helen stopped abruptly. 'Elsie had no right to say that,' she said sharply.

'Do I?' he insisted. 'Everyone else seemed to agree.'

Helen sighed and eyed him critically, knowing from the stubborn set of his jaw that he wasn't going to let it drop.

'Yes and no. He has a dimple in his chin like yours. And you're…' She searched for a word that wouldn't betray how utterly sexy she thought he was. 'Handsome…I guess, like he is…'

James laughed, which emphasised his dimple. 'Why, thank you.'

'It's probably more your persona. I think maybe she recognised the swagger, your confidence, the whole easy-rider look.'

'Are you close?'

Good question. Helen started walking again. 'I love him, sure. He's this larger-than-life kind of guy who sweeps into town on his Harley every once in a while and we talk and we laugh and it's just like old times, and then he starts to get that look in his eyes and I know he'll be leaving and…sometimes that's hard.'

'Hard because you don't know when you'll see him again?'

They were nearly back at the practice and Helen stopped and looked up at him. 'Hard because he chooses the road over me. Every time.'

She walked inside and left him standing on the pavement. The pain in her words grabbed at his gut. No wonder she had her feet planted firmly on the ground. He sensed her abandonment and it cut him like a knife.

Helen Franklin was definitely not a woman you could love and leave. She'd been through enough.

CHAPTER FOUR

HIS first week went well. The cumbersome cast was annoying and basic things such as walking, bathing and dressing were frustrating experiences, but his leg rarely ached any more. There had been the suspected influx into the practice and Thursday and Friday he was fully booked.

Living with Helen was an interesting experience. There'd been no more early morning incidents for which his sanity was grateful. In fact, outside work, he saw very little of her. A bit around the house as she flitted from one social engagement to the other but otherwise she was largely absent. He began to wonder if she was avoiding him.

She was polite, even invited him along to places, but he got the impression she was doing it only to be civil and the last thing he wanted to do was cramp her style. And the broken leg made everything just that little bit more difficult so he was content to stay at home. He loved to read and his enforced confinement gave him the perfect opportunity.

But even the most engrossing read couldn't block out the distracting presence of her in the house. Even absent, she was everywhere. Her rose perfume permeated everything. The lounge chair smelled like her, the cushions. The bathroom smelled like her and the cabinet was cluttered with her things. The house was cluttered with her things. Photos and mementos and ducks. Lots and lots of ducks. Wooden ducks, ceramic ducks, bronze ducks.

'Ducks?' he had said.

She had shrugged dismissively. 'I collect them. Have for years.'

A duck collector—definitely a homebody.

But it wasn't just her stuff. It was more. The way she hung the teatowels on the oven handle reminded him of her. The vase full of flowers on the dining-room table that she picked fresh from the garden every few days reminded him of her. Her chirpy message on the answering-machine made it hard to forget he was living in her house.

At night he'd let the phone ring until the machine picked it up. He told himself it'd be for her anyway but he suspected it was more to do with enjoying the sound of her voice even if it was on a tape.

By the week's end he was starting to go a little stir crazy, trapped in the house with her smell and her machine message and her bloody ducks. He wasn't used to this level of inactivity. Not having his bike and not being able to physically go for a ride whenever the whim took him was frustrating. He didn't like the feeling of being grounded. His itchy feet were almost as bad as the itch beneath his cast, which sometimes drove him quite mad.

Helen took pity on him on Sunday night. 'Come on,' she said. 'Get dressed. You've got ten minutes.'

He looked up from his book. She was wearing jeans that clung to her legs and a lacy button-up shirt with a V-neck in almost the exact shade of her nightdress. He could just see a glimpse of pink lace at her cleavage and he wondered if it was the same pink bra she'd been wearing the day she'd dragged him off the side of the road.

Her hair was down and had been brushed until it looked like burnished wood—sleek and lustrous. Her lips shone with a clear gloss and her green eyes were emphasised further by lashes accentuated with a coat of sooty mascara.

'Where are we going?'

'Trivia night at the pub.'

James stared at her. He seriously doubted he could go anywhere with her looking like that and not want to touch her. Maybe staying home was a better tactic.

Helen stared down at him, waiting for an answer. 'You need to get out and the team's down a player.'

When he still didn't do anything, she said, 'You don't like trivia?'

'Um, no, it sounds fun.'

She waited for him to move. When he didn't she gave an exasperated jiggle. 'You suck at trivia?'

He laughed. 'I can hold my own.'

'Good, 'cos we're winning. You now have…' she checked her watch '…eight minutes.'

James felt the last semblance of his good sense slip. He really did need to get out of the house. And should the desire to touch the much-grounded Helen Franklin overwhelm him, there'd be plenty of people around to discourage what was most definitely a very bad idea.

He hauled himself upright, using his crutches. 'Time me.'

Six and a half minutes later he swung into the lounge room. 'Will this do?'

Helen's breath caught in her throat. She always under-estimated his impact. His height and width were striking. His body dwarfed the crutches, making them look like spindly matchsticks.

He was wearing baggy denim shorts and a blue polo shirt almost the exact shade of his turquoise eyes. He'd brushed his unruly locks into a semblance of order but still his fringe did that endearing flop. His aftershave wafted towards her and she was overcome with the urge to bury her face in his neck.

Do? He was going to treble the pulse rate of every woman in the pub. 'Fine.' She nodded and briskly looked away. 'Let's go.' She grabbed her bag off the coffee-table. 'Normally I'd walk but we'll drive so you don't have to hobble too far.'

Helen was relieved when they arrived at the Drovers' Arms. James's presence in the house was unsettling enough—in the close confines of the car it was completely unnerving. Last time he'd been in her vehicle he'd been a safe distance away in the back. Having him sitting beside her, his large hand resting on his leg in her peripheral vision, his spicy fragrance drifting her way was a real test. She clutched the knob of the gear lever tightly and kept her eyes glued to the road.

There was a fair crowd inside the pub and a country rock song blared from the jukebox. Helen was grateful for the noise and distraction. Her team mates cheered when they spied her and waved her over.

'Do you want a drink?' James asked as they passed the bar.

'Diet cola,' she said, and left him to it. She didn't know how he was going to manage two drinks and his crutches and she didn't care. She needed space.

Of course, she needn't have worried. Glynis on the bar insisted on bringing the drinks to the table and fussed over him while he sat down. She batted her eyelids and patted James's shoulder sympathetically, her crimson-tipped nails like an exotic bird flying high against the plain blue of his shirt.

Helen rolled her eyes. Glynis was the only other single woman in town. She'd been in to see James on Thursday with some vague symptoms and had left grinning like a Cheshire cat. Still, half the town had been in to see him with vague symptoms so she could hardly single out Glynis for her displeasure.

James had taken the seat beside her and she was very conscious of his heat, his smell as he sipped at his beer. She introduced him to the rest of the team and then Alf took the small stage used for visiting bands and other acts and the evening commenced.

Helen was impressed. James was good. As good as she was. In fact, better than her tonight. His solid presence beside her was very distracting. Why couldn't he have been as dumb as a rock? He would have been much easier to dismiss.

Sure, she knew he was intelligent. He was a doctor. But she had often found that intelligence and general knowledge didn't always go hand in hand. She'd met a surprising number of doctors and other supposedly intelligent people whose general knowledge was rubbish. His, however, was brilliant.

James was enjoying himself. It felt good to be social- ising and everyone at the table had greeted him warmly. It was interesting to sit back and watch Helen interact with her friends. She was obviously well liked and, as leader of the team, no slouch at trivia either.

He motioned Glynis to bring him another drink. Beer was definitely required, sitting this close to her. When she laughed it went straight in his ear and her breasts bounced enticingly. Her arm rubbed against his occasionally and it took all his willpower not to slide his arm around her shoulders, glide his fingers through her hair.

There was a good mix at the table. Frank and his wife were there. He was sitting in for Genevieve. There was Bev, who worked as a receptionist at the nursing home, and then, interestingly, Skye's three bachelor boys. The vet, Graham. The paramedic, Tom. The pharmacist, Brendan. And they all seemed more than a little interested in Helen. Tom in particular. Every time James glanced down the end of the table, he was watching Helen. And if he wasn't watching her, Tom was keeping a close eye on him.

The evening drew to a close with the team—Helen's Heroes—staying at the top of the leader board.

'I can walk you home if you like, Helen,' Tom said as the group headed for the door.

'Thanks, Tom, but I've got the car so Hopalong…' she slapped James's cast as he swung past '…didn't have to walk too far.'

'Hey,' James protested, pulling up. 'Watch it. I'm not going to be Hopalong for ever.'

He grinned down at her and she grinned back. She'd touched up her gloss and her mouth looked very, very inviting.

Tom glared at him and James met his hostility without flinching and then turned and headed for the car. He felt sorry for the younger man. He looked about Helen's age and was living in a place where eligible women were as rare as hen's teeth. No wonder he was acting like a dog protecting an exceedingly juicy bone.

He waited in the car while she chatted with Tom. He heard her laughter and fought the urge to wind down the window and eavesdrop. It was none of his business who she talked to or what they said. Helen Franklin was none of his business, full stop.

Helen climbed into the car a few moments later. 'Well, you were a hit,' she said. 'I hope you had fun.'

Not much of a hit with Tom. 'I had a great evening.' He smiled.

She started the car and pulled away from the kerb. 'That question about the termite mounds—we wouldn't have got that without you. It was pretty obscure—how did you know about it?'

'I travelled all around the territory on my bike last year. The termite mounds up there are pretty amazing. I went through a stage where I read everything I could on them.'

'Well, thank you. Hope that head of yours is full of more useless trivia.'

He laughed. 'Now, there's a backhanded compliment if ever I heard one.'

She ignored him. 'Because we intend to win the cup for the third year in a row.'

He whistled. 'A hat trick.'

'That's the one.'

He looked at her and smiled. She smiled back. The amber flecks in her eyes glowed with zeal and her lip gloss glistened as passing streetlights accentuated the lustre. He looked away before he did something stupid. Like reach across and kiss her.

He had to fight this attraction at all costs. She couldn't give him what he needed—a casual affair. And he couldn't give her what she needed—a lasting relationship.

They pulled into the drive and Helen's hand shook slightly as she removed the keys from the ignition. She'd had such an enjoyable time and driving home with him seemed so very intimate. She had felt his gaze on her as she'd driven and she desperately needed air.

'So, you and Tom, huh?' James asked as he manoeuvred his leg and the rest of him out of the car.

Helen took a few gulps of cool, fresh air. 'What? Don't be ridiculous.'

James raised his eyebrows at her vehement reaction. 'Me thinks the lady doth protest too much.'

Helen felt her heart hammering. She didn't want to be talking about her love life with him. Again, it was too intimate. Something that people who knew each other really well did. She sighed. 'We're just friends. We went to school together. He's like a brother.'

James looked at her dubiously as he followed her into the house. 'You can't be that blind surely? I'm pretty sure he doesn't look at you as a sister. He fancies you like mad. In fact, all three of them seemed pretty interested.'

Helen was glad the darkness hid her blush. She'd been aware of the subtle competition between the men for her favour for quite a while. 'Well, I'm not,' she said briskly, heading to the door.

'Oh, yeah? Never even been on a date with one of them?' He hobbled along behind her.

'No.' She opened the door, flicked on the light and threw her bag down on a lounge chair.

James watched her from the doorway. He could see a faint tinge of pink in her cheeks. 'Have they asked?'

Helen kicked off her shoes and gave him an exasperated look. 'And this is your business, how?'

He grinned. 'Want a coffee?'

'If you're making.'

He swung past her on his crutches. 'Make the cripple do the work,' he teased.

Cripple? Even slightly incapacitated, he looked more virile, more capable than any man she'd ever met. 'I'll supervise.'

She followed him into the kitchen, his powerful triceps bunching and relaxing as he exerted his weight down through the crutch, his denim-clad butt taut as he supported his muscular frame on one leg.

James put his crutches to one side as he prepared the percolator, hopping occasionally and using the cupboards for support. Helen hiked herself up on the bench and watched him, idly swinging her legs. The coffee was dripping into the pot within minutes and the whole kitchen smelled divine.

'Mmm, I love that smell,' Helen said, inhaling deeply.

James turned and caught the very interesting expansion of her chest. 'Mmm,' he agreed. *Almost as good as you.*

He held her gaze for a long moment. She was beautiful. Her hair loose, her shapely legs swinging lazily.

'What?' she asked.

He shrugged, breaking eye contact as he took two mugs off the mug tree. 'I was just wondering how come one of those three eager guys hadn't managed to snare you.'

Because they didn't do anything for her. Because they didn't make her feel the way she felt when she was around him. All light-headed and giddy and like she was going to suffocate. Sure, she liked them but she wasn't ready to settle for lukewarm. Not yet.

She watched him pour steaming coffee into their mugs and add milk and sugar. 'It's difficult in a place like Skye. There's me and Glynis from the pub. And there are only three eligible men under forty. Few of the kids that grow up here ever stay. They head for the city. The bright lights. So when your choices are limited you start to see possibilities that you wouldn't have done if you'd had a wider choice.'

James slid her mug over to her. 'I don't think you're giving yourself much credit.'

She stared into the murky depths of her coffee, feeling suddenly depressed. She inhaled the aroma again, hoping for an instant pick-me-up. 'It's just the way it is.'

James slid his coffee along the bench too so he could stand closer to Helen. He stopped about a foot from her thigh and leaned a hip against the counter. 'So you're not interested in any of them?'

Helen blew on the scalding liquid and sipped. She may have been sitting on the bench but she still had to look up into his face. 'No. And they know that.'

Her voice was pensive and emphatic all at once. Her jade eyes were illuminated by the flecks of amber. James had his first real insight into dating in a small town. It obviously wasn't easy.

They sipped at their coffees for a while. James was acutely aware of her thigh a mere arm's length from him.

'I get the feeling,' he said after a few minutes, 'they're all just circling, though. Waiting for you to change your mind.'

Helen nodded. So did she. She gently swirled the contents of her mug. 'I probably will. Sooner or later.'

James almost choked on his mouthful. 'What? Why?' he demanded.

Helen was instantly annoyed at his tone. All right for Mr Wind-in-Your-Face, Easy-Rider. Mr Sex-on-Wheels, Girl-in-Every-Town. 'It's just practical,' she said defensively.

She had to be insane. Right? 'Practical? How?'

'I do want to marry, you know. Have children. If the right guy doesn't come along then I guess I'll have to take what I can get.'

James couldn't believe what he was hearing. 'Don't you want more? A grand love? I thought that's what every woman wanted.'

Helen snorted. 'I'd settle for someone who preferred me over the highway.'

'What about passion?' he pushed.

'Passion is overrated.' Her parents' union had apparently been highly passionately but it hadn't equipped them to cope with the day-to-day realities of life. With the sickness part of their wedding vows.

He gaped at her. 'Are you kidding? Passion is vital. Only someone who's never experienced true passion would say something so naive.'

'Hey,' she said, putting down her mug, 'just because I live in the sticks, it doesn't mean I haven't experienced passion. I did go to university, you know.'

James snorted and put down his mug. 'If it was anything like my uni years, it was more clumsy fumblings and sloppy kisses.'

'Yeah, well, don't judge me by your ineptitude.' Helen could feel her breath getting shallower, her voice getting huskier. She could see his chest rising and falling more quickly, hear the rough edge to his breathing. Suddenly the small kitchen felt positively claustrophobic.

How dared he imply she didn't know about passion? She'd had a six-month relationship with an ancient history student in her second year that had blown her socks off. They'd been nineteen and insatiable.

'Just because you're a lousy kisser.' She knew she was goading him but who the hell had died and made him master of all things passionate?

James had been called a lot of things in his life but a lousy kisser wasn't one of them. He noted the agitated rise and fall of her chest, the catch in her breath as she spoke. This conversation was totally ridiculous and he'd never been more turned on in his life. *Lousy kisser indeed. We'll just see about that.*

He put his hand on her thigh. 'Care to put that to the test?'

His touch was burning a hole in her jeans and Helen realised she had moved them into dangerous territory. His turquoise eyes were blazing with something she'd never seen before. But on some base level she knew what it was. Lust. Pure and simple. At nineteen there had been desire. This was more. This was grown-up. This was virile male animal ready to pounce.

She swallowed. Her heart tripped. 'James, I…'

He applied pressure through his hand and slid her petite body across the bench, easily obliterating the small space separating them. He put his hands on the bench on either side of her thighs, capturing her in one easy movement.

Their faces were close. He could feel her breath on his cheek, smell the coffee. 'You think I'm a lousy kisser?' he asked softly, staring at her mouth.

Helen swallowed again, her throat suddenly as dry as day-old toast. His mouth was so close, well and truly invading her personal space. She flicked her tongue out to moisten her lips and saw his pupils flare. 'I—'

His mouth descended on hers swiftly, cutting off her words. Her lips were soft and pliant and he plundered them in a brief, hard kiss.

'You were saying?' he asked, breaking away with the little willpower he had left.

Helen was breathing heavily, dazed and reeling from the onslaught. His lips were moist and she wanted them back on hers again. She wanted them everywhere.

'I—'

He cut her off again, claimed her mouth again and her moan went straight to his groin, stoking the heat raging there another degree or two. Her arms wound around his neck and he moved his hands from the bench to cup her backside. In one swift, bold movement he pulled her forward and gave a deep satisfied groan when her legs parted to cradle his hips.

His tongue demanded entry and she opened to him as she had opened her legs. He probed her mouth and her tongue danced with his, revelling in the taste of him. He pulled her against him harder and she could feel the ridge of his erection pressed against her.

Without conscious thought she wound her legs around him. His groan empowered her, the squeeze of his hands at the juncture of her buttocks and thighs emboldened her. Her hand snaked up into his hair as she rubbed herself against his hardness. His swift indrawn breath was dizzying.

Their breathing was the only sound in the room. But it was loud enough. Harsh gasps, desperate pants and flaring of nostrils sucking in much-needed oxygen. Just listening to the lack of control in his breath, the way his hand trembled as it pushed through her hair was making her hot.

In fact, she was hot all over. Hot and needy. She didn't want this kiss to end. She wanted to lie back on the bench, stretch out and let him kiss her all over. Afterwards she could plead temporary insanity but right now she wanted more.

The harsh jangle of the phone split the air. Helen pulled back from the kiss as abruptly as if someone had poured cold water on them.

'Leave it,' he said, breathing hard, dropping a chain of kisses down her neck.

She closed her eyes and felt the pull of his lips against

her skin. Oh, dear God, how had they ended up here? The phone rang despite her turmoil. 'No,' she said in a shaky voice, pushing against his chest. 'Let me down.'

James drew in a ragged breath, curled his hands into his pockets and stood back to give her her freedom. His heart pounded in his chest, his head spun and his groin ached as she walked away.

Helen strode into the lounge room. It was nearly eleven o'clock. The caller ID alerted her it was Elsie calling. *Good timing, Elsie.* She picked up the phone with shaking fingers.

'Elsie?'

There was silence at the other end but Helen was still a little distracted from the kiss.

'Elsie?'

Helen thought she heard some noise. A bit like heavy breathing. A prickle of alarm shot up her back, dissipating the sexual energy.

'Is that you, Elsie? Is everything all right?'

Still nothing. She hung up the phone and picked up her bag.

'What's up?' James asked, swinging into the room.

She glanced up at him and then wished she hadn't. His hair looked all tousled from where she had run her fingers through it and his gaze still smouldered with turquoise heat.

'Not sure,' she said briskly, searching around the bottom of her handbag for her keys. 'That was Elsie's number but when I answered there was silence.'

He frowned. 'Could it be a prank call?'

'Hardly. She's in her eighties.' She located her keys and slipped her shoes back on.

'Where are you going?'

'To Elsie's,' she said, heading to the door.

'It's eleven o'clock.'

'Exactly. Something's up.'

'There can't be too much up if she was able to dial your number.'

'I'm on speed dial, she'd only need to hit one button.'

'Call an ambulance, then,' he said, following her.

Helen stopped, her hand on the doorknob. 'I'm not going to get Tom out of bed until I know if he's required. If an ambulance pulled up only to find that Elsie's accidentally knocked the phone off the hook she'd be mortified to have wasted poor Tom's time and precious resources. I'll check on her first.'

'All right,' he said, following her outside.

'Where are you going?' she asked as she realised he was right behind her.

'With you.'

'There's no need,' she said.

'I'm not letting you go out in your car on the highway by yourself in the dead of night.'

Helen laughed. 'Well, thanks for being all proprietorial, but this is Skye.'

He shrugged. 'If something's happened, you'll need a doctor anyway, right?'

Helen weighed the pros and cons quickly. Having him in close confines after what they'd just shared was going to be awkward, but what if Elsie needed a doctor? She couldn't take the risk to save herself ten minutes of strained conversation with a man who had just kissed her senseless.

'Right.'

She climbed into the car and started the engine, pulling away as soon as James had shut his door. The silence built between them and Helen searched for an inane topic. But her head was too full of a hundred dire possibilities over Elsie and a blow-by-blow rerun of the kiss.

James cleared his throat. 'About before…'

Right. Yes. Good idea. Clear the air. Get in before he gave her the it-was-great-but-it-didn't-mean-anything spiel. 'It was a mistake. I know.'

It was. It definitely was. He'd made enough in his life to know. OK, usually they didn't make him feel this good but there was a first time for everything. 'Yes,' he said absently, trying to grapple with his buzzing body.

'You're here for four months. I'm a lifer. It doesn't matter how good it was—'

James turned to her. 'It was good, wasn't it?'

Oh, man, it had been incredible! She rolled her eyes. 'That's not the point.'

'Isn't it?'

'No,' she said, shooting him an exasperated look.

James had forgotten the point. 'What was the point?'

'I believe it was to prove that you weren't a lousy kisser.'

He chuckled. 'That's right. So?'

As her face flamed she refused to look at him. 'Look, I don't make out on kitchen benches. This isn't me.'

'Yeah, well, maybe you should.' He grinned. 'You're really good at it.'

Her toes curled traitorously in her shoes at his hearty compliment.

'That's not the—'

'Point,' he interrupted.

'You're leaving. That is the point. And I'm not going there.'

He sighed. She was right. He didn't do serious relationships. The only serious relationship he'd ever been exposed to had been his parents' and that had been enough to put him off for life. It was imperative he didn't let a mind-blowing kiss and a woman he barely knew negate hundreds of painful reminders.

'You're right, of course. And I will drop it. But only if you admit I'm a terrific kisser.'

She rolled her eyes at him. 'How old are you?'

He laughed. 'It's fair enough. A man has his pride. You called me inept. Lousy, even. You dented my ego.'

'Your ego needs a dent or two.'

He laughed again. 'Come on, Helen. Say it. I promise there'll be no more repeats for the rest of my stay. Just friends.'

'Friends? You promise?'

He nodded. 'Unless you beg me to take you, of course.'

He was grinning at her again and she smiled because his dimple made him look like a cheeky little boy. 'You're incorrigible.'

'I know.'

She stared at the road, her headlights illuminating the darkness. She took a deep breath. 'You're not a lousy kisser. There…I said it.'

'Can you give me a rating?'

She laughed. Typical male. He'd probably been rating women since he could count to ten. 'No, I can't.'

'Well, for what it's worth, I give you an eleven. That's the best damn kiss I've ever had.'

Helen blushed and concentrated really hard on not running the car off the road.

'I bet you say that to all the small-town girls,' she quipped.

His chuckle washed over her and she squirmed in her seat to quell the ache deep inside her. Four months stretched ahead as endlessly as the road in front of her.

CHAPTER FIVE

THE farm dogs were barking furiously by the time Helen pulled the keys out of the ignition at Elsie's. They ran towards the car in a pack, Shep, the blue cattle dog, leading. His threatening bark melted into whines of recognition as Helen called to him quietly.

'Hey, Shep, you're a good watchdog, aren't you, boy? Where's Elsie, boy? Is Elsie OK?' She bent down and gave the dog a scratch behind the ears.

Helen didn't wait for James, although she was aware of his crutches crunching on the loose gravel and his deep voice crooning a welcome to Shep. The sensor lights had come on and it was bright enough for him to see the way.

Now she was here, she was keen to check on Elsie. The door opened and a bleary-eyed Duncan gave her a confused look. 'Helen?'

'Evening, Duncan. Sorry to disturb you in the middle of the night. Is Elsie OK?'

Duncan frowned. 'Yes. She was fine when she went to bed.'

'I've just received a phone call from your number. She's

probably just knocked the phone off the hook but I thought I'd better check it out.'

Duncan's frown turned to worry and he stood aside to let his visitors in. Helen made a quick introduction and Duncan led the way through the house at a brisk pace. He didn't even knock on his grandmother's door but burst straight in.

'Gran!'

Helen heard his strangled exclamation before she'd even entered the room, and prepared herself for the worst. Elsie was lying on the floor on her back beside her bed, the telephone that usually sat on her bedside table sitting on her chest, one hand clutching the receiver.

'Gran, Gran.'

Duncan was down on the floor beside Elsie, shaking her shoulders, his distress evident.

Helen knelt beside him, pushing aside her own fear. She felt for and quickly found a weak carotid pulse. Elsie's eyes were wide open and Helen felt gutted at the frightened look there. You'll be all right, Elsie, everything will be fine, she wanted to say, but her heart sank at the very obvious droop to the right side of Elsie's face. She was drooling and her breathing was noisy.

No, no, no. Please, let her be OK.

'Call Tom,' she said to Duncan.

Duncan turned and looked at her as if she were an alien life form. She saw fear in his gaze and she could tell the last thing he wanted to do was leave. She understood. She may not share the same blood as Elsie, but she was as dear to Helen as she was to Duncan. Helen looked at the man she regarded as a brother, stricken by the grief she saw there. She wanted to hug him and weep into his shoulder.

'Duncan,' James said quietly but firmly, having quickly assessed the situation. 'Let Helen and I take care of her now. We need Tom here. I need you to ring him. Tell him Elsie's collapsed. Tell him I think it may be a CVA.'

Helen was grateful James had jumped in. Grateful too that he had chosen the correct medical terminology—cerebral vascular accident—rather than the colloquial term 'stroke'. She didn't want to panic Duncan or Elsie. Not yet. Knowing it herself was awful enough.

It was too hard to judge right now how extensive it was. The next few days would see swelling around the site in the brain where the stroke had occurred and it wasn't until it started to subside that they'd have a clearer picture of Elsie's recovery.

Duncan looked at Helen for confirmation. She nodded, pleased beyond words that James had insisted on accompanying her. She was too close to Elsie and her family, too worried about the old woman herself to be the person Duncan needed her to be. Strong and positive.

Duncan stirred himself. 'CVA…right,' he said.

'Use the phone outside,' James said, prising the receiver out of Elsie's hand and replacing it in its cradle. Elsie's bedroom wasn't exactly small but it wasn't palatial either and with he and Helen in here it was already crowded enough. 'It'll give us room to work.'

'Outside…right. Collapsed. CVA. Right.' Duncan left, still on autopilot, shock blunting his reactions. Helen hoped he remembered the information.

James lowered himself to the floor, gingerly using one crutch, his powerful arm muscles supporting his weight. He sat, his legs spread and outstretched on either side of Elsie's head. Helen shuffled over to make room for him.

'Hi, Elsie,' he said gently, smiling down at her. 'I was hoping we'd next meet over a lamb roast.'

Helen felt tears spring to her eyes at James's tenderness. She needed to pull herself together. She was of no use to Elsie if she was a blubbering mess.

James didn't like the older woman's colour. She was very pale and her lips had lost their pinkness. The stroke had obviously compromised her airway and he wanted her in a more manageable position. 'Elsie we're just going to roll you onto your side while we wait for Tom.'

He glanced at Helen and noticed the shimmer of tears in her eyes. He squeezed her hand and she seemed to visibly straighten then she nodded her readiness. Elsie was quite skinny and he knew they'd be able to manage her easily.

Elsie opened and shut her mouth a few times but no words came out, just gurgly vocal sounds. Her eyes bulged in fear.

'It's OK, Elsie, we're here now,' Helen reassured her, her heart breaking, unable to bear the anxiety she saw in Elsie's gaze. 'We'll take good care of you. Tom will be here soon.'

James supported Elsie's neck, protecting her C-spine in case she'd done any damage when she'd fallen. He counted to three and Helen rolled Elsie onto her left side. James wedged his broken leg against her back and spread his good leg further.

Helen felt more in control now and arranged Elsie's limbs into the recovery position, pulling the pillows off her bed to make it a little more comfortable.

'Put one under her head,' James said. He maintained neck support as he lifted Elsie's head so Helen could slip a pillow underneath it.

He was happy with the improvement in her lip colour and a reduction in her noisy breathing. He could still hear a faint rasp, however. And he was worried that if she vomited, a common occurrence post-CVA, the stroke might have knocked out her gag reflex, which existed primarily to protect the airway from aspiration. He'd have given anything for some oxygen and suction.

'Elsie, my love, I'm just going to hold onto your chin so your airway stays clear.'

He placed two fingers under Elsie's chin and gently lifted her jaw. The rasp disappeared and he was able to simultaneously monitor her carotid pulse with the same hand.

'Tom's coming,' Duncan announced from the doorway. Denise, his wife, was standing beside him.

After Tom's display in the pub earlier James would have been happy to never see him again, but now he was grateful. Elsie's pulse was rapid and weak—Tom couldn't get there fast enough.

'Is she going to be OK?' Duncan asked.

Helen looked at him and felt conflicted about what to tell him. She also wanted to be careful when she wasn't sure what Elsie could hear or understand. She wasn't sure she could open her mouth without crumpling into a heap.

James could see Helen's uncertainty. 'She's in good hands now,' James reassured him. 'We'll know more when we can do some tests.'

Duncan looked at James as if he was seeing him for the

first time. His shoulders sagged. 'Thanks, Doc. I don't know what we'd do without her.'

Helen was pleased that James's quick noncommittal reply had alleviated Duncan's worry. Pleased that it had let her off the hook. She'd been next to useless and she didn't know what she would have done without *him*.

They stayed by Elsie's side while they waited for Tom. Helen monitored her pulse and talked to her reassuringly. James maintained her airway. Denise packed a bag. Duncan paced outside the room, making frequent trips to the window, searching for the red and blue lights.

Tom arrived ten minutes later with an oxygen kit and a portable monitor. He greeted Helen warmly and gave James a curt nod. He assembled an oxygen mask and handed it to James to apply and passed the ECG electrodes to Helen to place on Elsie's chest.

They watched the screen as a heart rhythm appeared. She was tachycardic but the rhythm was essentially normal. Tom wrapped a blood-pressure cuff around Elsie's thin arm and pushed a button. The cuff pumped up automatically and they watched and waited for the number to appear on the screen. Two hundred and ten over one hundred and fifty.

'Does she have a history of hypertension?' James asked Helen.

She nodded. 'She's on a beta-blocker. It's always been well controlled.'

'Let's get an IV in before we move her,' James said.

Tom nodded and within a minute or two had efficiently placed one in the back of Elsie's left hand. Between the three of them they got Elsie onto a stretcher and bundled her into the back of the waiting ambulance.

'You go in the back with Elsie,' Helen told James.

'She'd probably prefer you,' Tom said stiffly.

Helen looked at Tom. She could tell he wasn't keen to have James in his vehicle. *Great!* Just what Elsie needed now was Tom in caveman role.

'He's a doctor, Tom,' she said, not bothering to keep the reproach out of her voice. 'And he has a broken leg. He can't drive the car back to Skye.'

Tom stared for a moment then nodded stiffly. 'Fine.'

James raised an eyebrow at her as Tom stalked back into the house. He grinned. 'Better not tell him about the kiss.'

'This is not funny,' she said sternly. She obviously needed to have another talk to Tom.

'No, of course not.' He grinned again.

She rolled her eyes. 'Get in.'

He chuckled and saluted. 'Yes, ma'am.'

Given the limited space, getting into the back of an ambulance wasn't easy at the best of times, but trying to do it on one leg was especially challenging.

'I'll take your crutches with me and follow you in,' Helen said once he'd lowered himself into the seat next to Elsie's stretcher.

James saluted again. 'Yes, ma'am.'

She shut the back doors on his grinning face and the heat in his turquoise eyes. *Damn the man to hell.* He said that so sexily. She wanted to climb in with him and pick up where they had left off.

When Tom emerged from the house a few minutes later she was still standing with her fingers on the handle, staring at the ambulance doors. 'You OK?' Tom asked, touching her arm lightly.

After tonight she seriously doubted whether she'd ever be right again. Between that kiss and Elsie, things had changed for ever.

She looked down at where Tom's hand rested. Nothing. She felt nothing. James just had to look at her with heat in his eyes and she could barely think straight. She roused herself. 'No, Tom. I'm not. I'll see you there.'

It was around one in the morning before they finally made it back home. They'd stayed until after Elsie's CT scan and bloodwork had come back. The diagnosis of stroke was confirmed, with a clot evident on the left side of her brain. It wasn't as extensive as they had feared and she was being administered a special clot-dissolving medication as they left.

The smell of coffee hit her as soon as she opened the door and Helen remembered she hadn't even turned the percolator off before they'd left. She headed for the kitchen. Their half-full coffee-mugs sat on the bench. She stared into the cold murky depths of her mug and remembered why they'd been discarded. Her cheeks grew hot just thinking about it.

'Want another coffee?' James asked from the doorway.

Helen shook her head, collected the mugs and placed them in the sink, emptying their contents and filling them with water. 'I'm going to hit the sack.'

She didn't look at him. She'd barely spoken in the car. James could tell she was taking Elsie's stroke hard. 'Are you OK?' he asked softly as he moved closer.

She nodded. 'Fine.'

'You don't seem fine.'

She shrugged. 'I'm just sad about Elsie. She's such a proud woman, she's going to hate being incapacitated in any way.'

James nodded. 'Will they be able to care for her at home?'

'I'm not sure.' Helen's brow furrowed. 'They both work long hours on the farm. It will depend on how much care she needs, I guess.'

It was hard to tell from the CT scan and James knew they wouldn't have a clearer picture for a few more days. 'Is there a waiting list at the nursing home?'

'Not usually.' Helen dried her hands, pushed away from the sink and flipped the switch on the percolator. 'Do you want one?' she asked.

'I'll get it,' he said, swinging closer to her.

Helen let go of the percolator. He was very near now and she could feel his heat encompass her. His shoulders were broad in her peripheral vision and she had a sudden desire to lay her head against his chest.

Elsie's plight was turning over and over in her mind and she wanted to cry for the proud old matriarch who had been part of the land and the town for over eighty years. She'd run the farm single-handedly after her husband had died and her three boys had still been toddlers. Not being able to communicate or feed, wash or go to the toilet herself would be the ultimate indignity for such an independent lady.

Her heart was so heavy Helen didn't think she could bear it. She desperately wanted to feel James's arms around her. Seek a little solace. A little comfort. But how would a man who had no roots anywhere understand her despair?

James lifted a hand and gently removed a lock of hair that had fallen across her downcast face. 'I'm sorry,' he whispered.

She looked up into his face and his breath caught. The amber flecks in her eyes were glowing with unshed tears. She was beautiful and so very sad and he wanted to pull her into his arms. But her gaze was also wary and her fingers were gripping the bench so hard her knuckles were white. She'd made herself very clear earlier and she'd been right.

Helen blinked rapidly. She nodded. 'Thanks.' And with every ounce of willpower she possessed she unfurled her fingers, skirted around his bulk and left the kitchen.

James poured himself a coffee, leant against the bench and pondered the two faces of Helen Franklin he'd seen tonight. Hot and moaning into his mouth. Heavy-hearted and serious. Curiously, both of them made him want more.

Much to everyone's delight, Elsie improved dramatically over the next fortnight. She'd been left with slight weakness to her right hand and leg and her speech, which had initially been very difficult to understand, improved every day until there was only a slight slur.

She was having daily sessions with the physio and speech therapist, and the occupational therapist had already made a house call at the farm to see what modifications could be made in preparation for her return home.

Two days after Elsie was admitted to hospital the heavens opened. Torrential rain fell relentlessly on the thirsty landscape, turning browns to greens and dry creek beds to lively waterways. Everyone agreed it was nature's way of encouraging Elsie back to the farm. As with all farmers, rain, or the lack of it, was a constant concern in their daily battle against the elements. The township of Skye felt sure that the rain would put a real spring in Elsie's step.

Often when Helen went to visit, she'd find James already there. He always left as soon as she arrived but the stroke hadn't knocked out Elsie's matchmaking centre—in fact, it seemed to have intensified it.

Elsie had an even greater sense of urgency, having faced her mortality once, and the hints she dropped were becoming more and more obvious. Not even the continuing rain that drummed loudly on the corrugated-iron roof of the hospital or her impending day release for her eighty-first birthday party could keep Elsie's mind off getting Helen and James together.

Despite Elsie's urgings, they hadn't had another incident like on the night Elsie had had her stroke. Thankfully James had kept his promise to just be friends and Helen was grateful for that. She really was. She'd had enough on her mind, worrying about Elsie, without any strange sexual vibe at home. In fact, it had been great, just kicking back and relaxing with him in the evenings. They took turns at cooking and they honed their trivia skills by watching television game shows.

It was just like the last time she'd had a house guest. Craig had been a learner GP on country rotation and had spent two weeks at the practice and boarding at the residence. The company had been good and it had been nice to have someone to talk to. Of course, he'd been fifty, married, balding and overweight, with a dreadful habit of picking his toenails, but apart from that it was practically the same.

Helen was sure that when James hit the big five zero his thick dark wavy locks would be starting to thin, too. His powerful leg muscles would, no doubt, have started to atrophy. His washboard abs turned a little soft—more jelly than jut. And his turquoise gaze would have lost its smouldering intensity, the chin dimple its boyish charm. No man could look that good for ever.

Two weeks after she'd left the farm in an ambulance, Elsie arrived back—even if it was just for the day. Helen, Denise and Duncan had gone all out, the homestead was decked out in balloons and streamers and all the old gumtrees sported yellow ribbons. Elsie was going to get a party to remember!

As they drove Elsie out to the farm James marvelled with her how much the landscape had been transformed by the rain. Water lay everywhere. Every depression was now a puddle or a small pond. The river that the highway out of Skye passed over, which had been no more than a muddy pond when he'd arrived, now ran so vigorously beneath the bridge that James felt sure he could lean over the railing and touch it.

The entire population of Skye clapped as Helen pulled up in the car and Alf hurried forward to help Elsie from the vehicle. The township had laid on quite a spread and Elsie beamed with joy at everyone as she sat in her wheel-chair like a queen receiving foreign dignitaries.

A marquee had been set up in the back yard and people mingled in small groups all happy to still have Elsie around for another birthday. Children darted in and out of the groups and Elsie clapped excitedly at their squeals of delight.

The rain had stopped momentarily and a few meek rays of sunlight pushed through the leaden sky. A brilliant rainbow shone over the farm and raindrops dripped from leaves and flowers and clung to spider webs.

James watched the scene as only a newcomer could. The dynamics of the town were fascinating and no more evident than at a celebration. He kept an eye on Helen as he mingled. She was wearing a black and white dress that clung in all the right places and he'd thought nothing but indecent thoughts ever since she'd put it on. Her hair was caught back in its usual ponytail and he itched to pull it out and let it tumble to her shoulders.

He'd been standing for an hour, leaning on his crutches, and his leg was starting to ache a little. Three weeks down the track the pain was non-existent for the most part. But if he stood for long periods of time it niggled away, letting him know he should sit down and put it up.

He felt a familiar well of frustration rise inside him. The leg had well and truly grounded him in Skye. Not that it had been a particular hardship but he'd never gone a month without riding his bike before and he could feel the gypsy in him urging him on.

He was impatient to get out and see some of the surrounding countryside. There were supposed to be some great thermal springs nearby and he yearned for a night under the stars with the crackle of a campfire keeping him company.

Helen had offered to take him sightseeing but he had

declined. He wanted to be on his bike, the wind in his face. It gave him such a different perspective to being cooped up in a car. He really wanted to witness firsthand the transformation of the scenery with the recent rain.

As soon as the cast came off he was heading out. He hadn't used his camera in over a month and he knew he'd get some spectacular shots of the land metamorphosing from brown to green. From slow death to vibrant life.

James wandered away from the groups of chatting locals. His crutches sank into the soaked grass, making his progress a little slower. The noise slowly receded as he made his way around the side of the low-set house and disappeared altogether as he reached the front.

He spotted a couple of chairs adorning the front patio and he gratefully lowered himself into one and propped his cast up on the other. He shut his eyes and sighed as the niggle eased immediately.

He opened his eyes and they came back into slow focus on the pond that dominated the circular driveway. He had commented to Helen on the way past today that he hadn't remembered seeing it the night of Elsie's stroke.

'You didn't,' she'd said.

She'd explained that years ago, back in its heyday, even before Elsie's time, the farm had had a large fountain adorning the entrance. After a series of hard-hitting droughts it had been deemed to be a waste of water and dug out. The intention had been to fill the hole in but generations of farm kids had used it to play in and it had been everything from a sandpit to a racetrack for toy cars.

Duncan's boys had a very elaborate system of jumps set up within it. Its depth and width and sloping sides made it perfect for them to practise their skateboard skills. But with the recent rain it had filled to overflowing and the only things benefiting from it at the moment were the ducks.

James's gaze settled on an object in the middle. It was white and quite bulky. It took a few seconds for his brain to work out what it was. A sick feeling washed through him and he stood abruptly as he realised. It was clothing. It was a person. Floating face down.

His heart thundered as his powerful arms propelled the crutches back and forth, back and forth. The wet ground grabbed at the rubber stoppers. How long had the person been immersed? As he drew closer he could see it was a child. How long? How long? Was it too late?

He reached the edge and threw his crutches to the ground, balancing on one leg. He looked down at the cast and knew it was about to become soaked and useless. He heard a noise behind him and he looked back. It was Duncan's twelve-year-old son.

'There's a kid fallen in the pond!' he yelled. 'Get Helen! Get Tom!'

James didn't stop to see if Cameron had obeyed him. He turned straight back to the water and hobbled in. On his stomach his hands could just reach the murky bottom and he propelled himself along, reaching the floating child in seconds.

He turned the little boy over and dragged him back to the edge. He could feel dampness permeating his cast and his leg weighed a ton. He felt frustrated he couldn't easily lift the child from the water and stagger out. He couldn't properly bear weight on his leg so he had to place the child on the ground and half crawl, half drag himself out.

The boy looked about five. His lips were blue, he was cold. James knew everything depended on quick and vigorous resuscitation and how long the child had been not breathing and without a pulse.

James ignored the pounding of his heart and the possibility that he was too late and found the calmness inside that honed his thought processes and sharpened his skills. Lying on his stomach, he grasped the boy's chin, pinched his nose and administered a gentle puff into his mouth.

'James!'

He heard Helen calling him, was conscious of shouts and people coming closer.

'Oh, God, its Josh, Alf's grandson. What happened?' Helen asked, throwing herself on the ground next to him. Josh was always in some scrape or other. He had a fairly thick chart back at the surgery to prove it. But this was extreme even for Josh.

'Don't know. I found him floating in the pond,' he said between puffs. 'Do compressions.'

Helen's hand shook as she ripped opened Josh's sodden shirt and performed quick compressions.

'Where's Tom? We need his kit.'

'He's gone for it,' Helen said.

James could hear a woman sobbing hysterically and guessed it was Josh's mother. She was desperately trying to get to him and people were holding her back so they could work. He tuned her out.

Helen could feel how cold Josh's skin was and knew they stood a better chance of resuscitating him if he was warmer. 'Denise, we need towels and blankets,' she said, not looking up from her task.

'How long's he been missing—does anyone know?' James asked Helen.

'Val thinks only a few minutes at the most.'

James nodded and puffed in more air. He hoped so. The shorter the time in the water, the better his chances. *Come on, Josh, breathe damn it.*

Just as Tom arrived and threw his kit on the ground beside them Josh started to dry-retch and then to cough. A stream of dirty water fountained from his mouth and seeped out of his nose. Helen and James rolled him quickly on his side. Josh took a couple of deep breaths and then opened his mouth and cried a long lusty cry.

The collective sigh of relief from the crowd was audible. Val was released and she threw herself down on the ground and scooped a bawling Josh up into her arms. Denise arrived back and threw a blanket around the bewildered child and the sobbing mother.

James felt his shoulders sag as the tension ebbed. He was still lying on his stomach and he dropped his head momentarily, feeling relief wash through his system.

Helen felt a surge of relief swamp her, too, and looked down to where James was lying. The dark wavy hair on his downcast head tempted her and she didn't bother to stop the urge that overcame her. He'd just saved a child's life. She ran her fingers through his glorious waves. 'Are you OK?' she asked.

James felt his scalp tingle as her fingernails grated erotically. He took a deep breath and raised his head, displacing her hand. 'I am now.'

She nodded and they smiled huge relieved smiles at each other. 'Come on.' She stood and picked up his discarded crutches from the ground, her dress wet and muddy. 'You're muddy, soaked and your cast is useless. You're going to need another one.'

He rolled on his back and sat up. Several of the men from the assembled crowd came forward and pulled him to a standing position.

There was much congratulating, backslapping and tearful cheek-kissing. Helen slipped him his crutches and then stood aside and watched a bemused James accept the thanks of the people of Skye.

'A hero. A bloody hero,' a choked-up Alf said as he vigorously shook James's hand.

Helen returned her attention to a mollified Josh. Tom had some oxygen running and was advising Val to take Josh to the hospital for a once-over. Helen supported Tom and Val agreed reluctantly. Helen could tell she wasn't going to let Josh out of her arms or sight for a very long time.

She glanced back at James. He was wet and muddy, his hair hanging in scraggily strips. But he was laughing at something Alf said and his dimple winked at her. His broad shoulders, flat stomach and slim hips clearly visible through his sodden clothes made her stomach muscles clench. And he had saved a little boy's life. And, damn it all, if it didn't look like he belonged here. He looked for all the world like he was one of them.

'All right, everybody, break it up, enough of the hero-worship. He won't be able to get his head through the door.'

There was general laughter and the crowd broke up. 'You've blown it now. They're never going to let you leave,' she said, watching the retreating backs of the towns-folk.

He chuckled. Somehow the thought didn't bother him so much. Maybe it was the elation of a good outcome or maybe it was her standing before him, mud on her dress, hair escaping her prim ponytail. But he had a real sense of home, of belonging for the first time in his life. 'There are worse things.'

She could see the heat in his turquoise gaze and suddenly she was back on the kitchen bench, her legs wrapped around his waist.

'Remind me of that when there's no more room in the fridge come tomorrow.'

He raised an eyebrow at her.

'Skye likes to feed its heroes.'

He grinned. 'Just as well I have a good appetite.'

She curled her fingers into her palms as reminders of his appetite scorched her insides. She forced her legs to move. 'Come on, then, hero. There's a plaster saw some-where with your name on it.'

He turned and watched her walk away, the two muddy patches covering her rear swaying hypnotically. He felt more than a little turned on at the thought of her packing a power tool.

He so liked a woman who was into DIY.

CHAPTER SIX

HELEN and James didn't bother shopping or cooking for the next two weeks. As she had expected, the good people of Skye had provided. A steady stream of gourmet dishes arrived morning and night. James flattered each offering and its bearer outrageously as they arrived and earned himself an even more elevated status in the community.

'You are shameless,' Helen said, shaking her head after she'd watched him flirt with Lola from the post office one morning.

James held the apple pie up to his face and inhaled the just-out-of-the-oven aroma. 'The least I can do is show my appreciation for such generosity,' he said with faux injured innocence.

'Appreciation? Lola practically melted into a puddle at your feet.'

He grinned. 'Is there something wrong with making a woman feel good about herself?'

His dimple taunted her and she rolled her eyes.

'What?' He chuckled. 'Can I help it if I have a way with women?'

'Oh, yeah,' she teased. 'You've got the grandmothers eating out of your hand.'

James remembered the heat of her mouth against his. *Not just the grandmothers.* He smiled. 'I seem to recall a certain registered nurse who had a little trouble keeping her hands off me.'

Helen's breath stopped in her throat at his cheeky reminder. Her thoughts froze. It took a second for her higher functions to return. 'A temporary aberration, I can assure you. Your charm may have every woman with a pulse in Skye all aflutter but you can save it with me, James Remington. I don't charm that easily.'

James laughed. 'I've noticed.'

His newfound hero status soon became a little overwhelming. People, strangers, thanked him in the street. His drinks were bought for him at the pub. The *Skye Herald* ran a story on him. The local schoolchildren from Josh's class sent him a poster with his picture from the paper stuck in the centre and 'Our Hero' in bold print at the top.

The community embraced him enthusiastically, like a long-lost son. He'd never felt so adored in his life. It was a total revelation for him. He'd locumed in small towns before but Skye had welcomed him with open arms.

He supposed, aside from Josh, his leg had a lot to do with it. It was harder to stay aloof from the dynamics of the town when he couldn't easily escape it. Not that he'd deliberately kept himself aloof in other places but he had been able to roam away on weekends to explore the local area—and he had. Here he was grounded and when he walked down the street, everyone knew him.

It felt surprisingly good. They were fine people with hearts of gold and their pleasure at seeing him was always genuine. Everywhere he went and everything he did, a strong sense of community prevailed. From the chook raffles at the pub on Sunday night to the friendly Friday night footy competition to the monthly barn dance, Skye thrived on its kinship.

James had never really felt like he'd belonged anywhere. But as Skye embraced him he began to feel a connection. Sure, he was dying to get on his bike and go for a ride. Longing to feel the wind in his face again. But he wasn't as stir crazy as he'd expected to be and his affection for Skye was growing each day.

Alf had made fixing James's bike his highest priority, ringing the Melbourne firm daily to check on the progress of the parts he required and not working on any other job for two days when they finally arrived. And if anyone in Skye grumbled about being bumped, his sharp 'It's for the doc' silenced any criticism.

As far as Alf was concerned, nothing was too much or too good for the man who had pulled his grandson's limp body out of the water and resuscitated him. James spent an hour or so after work each day at the garage, checking on progress and talking engines, and Alf was more than happy to chat with the man who had saved Josh.

Yes, his time in Skye was very pleasant indeed. Except for Helen. His attraction for her didn't seem to lessen with time, no matter how much he told himself it wasn't going to happen. If anything, it seemed to get stronger.

He smelt roses wherever he went. A faint trace of them clung to his clothes, reminding him of her even when she wasn't around. Her ponytail swished enticingly and although she was very careful, he caught the occasional glimpse of her in her sleep shirt.

Once he'd even come home after being at Alf's and caught her coming out of the kitchen munching on an apple, swathed in a purple bath towel, a white one tied turban-style around her hair. Her shoulders had been bare except for the occasional water droplet.

They had both frozen on the spot and stared for what had seemed like for ever. It had taken all his willpower not to move towards her. He had apologised and she had fled the room. They hadn't spoken about it since, but he had dreamt about it often. Too often for his own sanity.

The day finally arrived for James to have his cast removed and he was awake early, raring to go. It was a beautiful Saturday morning and as he swung his legs out of bed he rapped on the cast with his knuckles.

'Not going to miss you, buddy.'

He had taken possession of his newly fixed bike a few days before and had already planned a day trip for tomorrow. He'd noticed a helmet in the garage when he'd been stowing the bike. He recognised it as Helen's from the photos of her and her father and he planned on asking her to accompany him.

He got up and put a pot of coffee on and waited impatiently for Helen to get up. The hospital was on the northern outskirts of town, a little too far to hobble, and she had told him she'd drop him there. He read for a while, got up and poured himself another cup, flicked on the television, turned it off and picked up his book again.

When she emerged at eight o'clock he almost leapt up and kissed her. Even her prim ponytail didn't register.

'You're ready, I see.' She smiled.

The curve of her mouth was as cute as hell. 'For two hours.'

'Can I get a coffee first?'

James suppressed the urge to scream. 'Of course. Half an hour's not going to be here or there.'

Helen downed a cup and they were at the hospital twenty minutes later. She accompanied him inside as she wanted to talk to Jonathon about Elsie, who was being discharged in the next few days.

She left James at X-ray and went in search of the med super. It was bedlam inside and when she finally tracked a nurse down twenty minutes later she was chatting to James.

'We won't be able to get to you for another half an hour or so, James,' she said, looking very harried. 'Sorry, we're down two nurses and Jonathon and the registrar are in Theatre, operating on a ruptured appendix.'

James bit down on a disappointed curse. 'That's OK,' he said. 'I don't want to be a bother. My X-ray's fine. Just give me the saw and I'll remove it myself.'

The nurse exchanged a look with Helen.

'James,' Helen said, 'don't be ridiculous. Removing it yourself will be too tricky.'

He nodded calmly. 'Tricky, but not impossible.'

She took pity on him. 'I'll do it,' she sighed. 'Get up on the table.' She left to get the plaster saw.

He grinned at her when she arrived back. She switched it on and the air filled with a loud mechanical whine. It looked like a bar mix with a round disc attachment. Helen watched the serrated edges agitate back and forth.

He pulled his shorts leg up close to his groin. 'Be gentle with me.'

He had said the same thing to her the first day they'd met and she shot him a withering look as she donned clear plastic glasses. She started at his toe and made her way up his leg. The sharp, tiny teeth made slow progress, kicking up fine plaster dust as they went, and it was too noisy for conversation. Which was just as well. Helen resolutely tried to ignore the fact that she was getting closer and closer to a region of him she'd tried not to think about for the last six weeks.

She didn't let her gaze wander up his leg further than it needed to, concentrating instead only on one patch of white at a time. As she got closer to her goal she realised what James without a cast meant. He would be mobile. Freer. No doubt she'd hardly see him at all now after his enforced respite.

Which was good. Really, it was a good thing. The less time he spent swanning around the house, looking all male and gorgeous, was a bonus. It was bad enough that every corner of the house held reminders of him. A pile of his books lying on the table beside his chair. A pot of percolating coffee every morning. The smell of his spicy aftershave ingrained into the curtains and the carpet and the fabric of the lounge cushions.

James off on his bike would be a good respite for her, too. He was kind of hard to ignore around the house and she was getting far too used to having him around. She found herself looking forward to the evenings as she sat at her desk each day. They ate and laughed and tried to outdo each other on the game shows or just sat in their lounge chairs and read. It was too companionable. Too cosy. It made her want things she couldn't have. She was pleased that it was coming to an end. Six weeks of enforced intimacy was more than enough.

Helen took off her protective glasses. 'Nearly there,' she said. 'Hang tight.'

James chuckled. Again, where could he go with a half-removed cast?

Helen picked up the spreaders, which looked like a giant pair of scissors with flat noses and long industrial-looking handles. She inserted the blunt blades into the furrow made by the saw and pulled down on the handles. The furrow widened, the plaster cracking a little as it split apart.

She repeated the process all the way back up his leg until the cast had been split wide open. She held onto the sides of the shell as he gingerly removed his leg.

'Oh, that feels so-o-o good,' James groaned, rubbing his hands up and down his freed leg. The leg looked ridiculously white compared to his other one, and he couldn't wait to get some sun on it. He grabbed Helen by the shoulders, pulled her close and laid a kiss on her lips. 'Thank you.'

He set her away from him again immediately and returned his attention to the leg. Helen hung onto the table as the brief contact with his mouth sent a shock wave through her body. She knew it was gratitude, pure and simple, that there had been no sexual intent, but it had rocked her nonetheless.

She faded out for a second and when she refocused he was scratching his leg.

'Hell, it feels good to be able to scratch it,' he muttered. 'It was always so damn itchy.'

Helen nodded absently. It was a common complaint. Before she could give it any serious thought her hand was on his lower leg, helping him scratch. It wasn't anything different to what she'd have done for any patient. She could feel the bulky contours of his calf twitch beneath her ministrations. 'Your muscles don't seem too wasted,' she commented.

James almost groaned out loud as her nails scraped against his skin. To be able to finally scratch the area felt wonderful but beneath her nails it was intensely pleasurable. He suddenly knew how a dog felt when the sweet spot behind its ears was hit and it would collapse to the ground in total ecstasy. He just wanted to roll his eyes and pant.

He swallowed. 'They could do with a little work.'

She frowned and knocked his hand out of the way to scrutinise his quad. She ran her hand over the thigh muscle, feeling its well-defined shape. Most men she knew didn't have even half the bulk. She could feel it tense as her fingers stroked over its outline.

'Still not bad for six weeks of no weight-bearing.' She looked at James and was startled to find his eyes shut and his head thrown back. Her hand stilled on his thigh, its bulk suddenly hot beneath her palm.

His eyes flickered open and she was lanced by the heat and desire in his smouldering turquoise eyes. Her mouth went dry as their gazes locked. She suddenly became very conscious of where her hand was and what she'd been doing. And how very un-nurse-like it was. How very unprofessional.

'I…I'm sorry,' she said, her voice husky. 'I…shouldn't have… I was just trying to…'

The rasp in her voice went straight to his already aching groin. 'I liked it,' he said, his voice soft and a little raspy also. *I was hoping you'd go higher.*

'It was…inappropriate,' she faltered. She removed her hand from his thigh and took a step back.

'We're attracted to each other, Helen. This is what happens when you deny it.' There, he'd said it. They'd both been pretending for too long.

No. She shook her head. 'It won't happen again.'

He nodded. He knew she was right. Crossing that line was not an option. 'I know,' he whispered.

Helen wanted to turn and run from the look of hunger in his eyes, but it was strangely compelling. She seemed fixed to the spot.

'Looking good, James,' a nurse called as she bustled by.

He smiled and waved and watched as Helen emerged from her trance-like state. The unsuspecting nurse had effectively thrown a bucket of cold water over the flames between them.

Helen took another step back. 'I'll go and see if Jonathon's out of Theatre yet,' she said, and fled.

Helen slept till late on Sunday morning. She'd been awake half the night thinking about the cast incident and wondering where James was. She hadn't seen him since practically molesting him and had noticed his bike had been missing from the garage on her return home a few hours later. He certainly hadn't wasted any time.

And why would he have? She'd probably come across as a gauche small-town girl who hadn't seen a well-built man in her life. So, he was attracted to her but he was also a gypsy at heart and she cringed at how she had pawed his leg and how desperate it must have seemed. She'd probably made him feel trapped. Suffocated.

She'd heard him get in around one a.m. Where had he been? Who had he been with? The questions had roared around in her brain despite knowing that the answers weren't any of her business. It had been another two hours until she had finally nodded off.

It was tempting to just stay in bed and hope he would go out again but hiding from the problem wasn't going to make it go away and they still had ten more weeks of being together. She dragged herself out of bed, dressed and steeled herself to clear the air.

A few moments later she found James preparing food in the kitchen. She watched him from the doorway for a while. It seemed strange to see him walking on both legs and stranger still to see him in jeans. They outlined his legs to perfection and she was reminded again how well defined his muscles were.

He seemed to be favouring his broken leg a little. 'Is it giving you trouble?' she asked.

James turned around. He hadn't seen her since yesterday morning and wasn't prepared for the impact of her ponytail and green-eyed gaze. 'Morning, sleepyhead.' He smiled. 'Thought you country girls were early risers.'

'Sleeping in isn't purely the domain of city chicks,' she

said dryly, pushing herself away from the doorframe and heading for the coffee-pot.

She poured herself a cup, conscious of his stare. 'So is it?' she asked turning to face him. 'Giving you trouble?'

He grimaced. 'No. Not really. I guess after having it so well supported for six weeks I'm still a little wary of putting my whole weight on it.'

Helen nodded. 'That's common enough. You'll conquer that the more you use it to bear weight.'

James nodded. They sipped at their coffees for a little while. Helen felt her heart pick up its tempo as she contemplated her next words until it thumped loudly in her chest. Surely he could hear it?

She stared into her coffee and cleared her throat. 'About yesterday.'

'Helen.'

She kept her gaze firmly fixed on the contents of her mug. 'It was very unprofessional—'

'Helen, you weren't removing my cast in your capacity as a nurse. You were doing me a favour.'

'Still…I shouldn't have touched you the way I did.'

'Not even if I wanted you to?'

Helen swallowed and ignored his question and what it did to her breathing. Thinking about him wanting her to touch him was not what she needed right now. 'What you said yesterday was right. I am attracted to you. But you should know that I'm not going to act on it.'

As James felt his body react to her statement he realised there was a major disadvantage to wearing jeans. Suddenly he yearned to be back in the baggy shorts the cast had forced him to wear. 'Because?'

'Because you'll be gone before too much longer and I'm over being left-behind girl.'

He regarded her seriously. 'I don't know how to be staying-put guy.'

Helen nodded. 'Exactly. That's why we can't do this.'

He knew she was right but…he wanted her. 'And you think it's possible to deny your body such a strong attraction?'

She shot him a scornful look. 'I'm an adult, James. Not some hormone-ridden teenager.'

James raised his eyebrows. 'I don't think it works like that.'

'Of course it does,' she scoffed. 'We have ultimate control over what we do.'

Something told James that Helen hadn't had a lot to do with intense physical attraction. He was one of the most controlled people he knew but one look at that damn ponytail and he wanted to rip her clothes off. *She had no idea.*

'So,' he said as he pushed away from the bench and slowly stalked towards her, 'when we get close like this…' he stopped in front of her '…and all we want to do is fall on each other, you want us to just ignore it?'

She felt suffocated as the breadth of his chest filled her vision and his words ignited a flame that licked her insides. Heat suffused her body. But she looked him square in the face. 'Yes.'

He stepped closer until their bodies were almost touching. 'And when our hands accidentally brush and all we can smell is each other and I know if I kiss your neck that your hair is going to brush against my face and you're going to sigh like you did that night right here on the bench behind me, you want us to ignore that, too?'

Helen could feel his heat as she remembered that night. Remembered how she'd wanted him closer. Wanted him inside her. Her internal muscles clenched as if he had entered her. She gripped the bench hard to stop from melting into a puddle at his feet.

This was a test and he had to know she meant what she said. 'Of course. All it takes is a little self-control.' Her voice didn't sound like her voice but she returned his gaze unwaveringly.

'Self-control. So working together, living under the same roof, sharing meals and a living area, sleeping with just a wall between us, that's all OK? Feeling our blood stir, our hearts…' he pressed two fingers lightly against the pulse fluttering frantically in her neck '…race when we're in the same room, you can just ignore it?'

His fingers slid down to the hollow at her throat and she swallowed. With a supreme effort she pulled his fingers away. 'Yes.'

He smiled. He could see the struggle lighting the amber flecks in her eyes. 'Prove it.'

Helen rolled her eyes and moved away from him, placing her mug in the sink. Released from the magnetism of his closeness, she heaved in some deep breaths. 'If you think I'm going to play truth or dare or some other juvenile game then think again.'

He chuckled as he thought about the things he could dare her with. 'No, nothing like that. All I ask is that you spend the day with me. I'm going out on the bike to the thermal pools. Come with me. Convince me you can get through a whole day without feeling the need to ravish me then I'll bow to your higher power and we'll play it your way.'

Helen wanted to spend the day with him like she wanted a hole in the head. Spending a couple of hours snuggled into his back would be temptation enough without further hours in his company. The more time she spent with him the stronger the attraction grew. She needed to limit their time together. Particularly their time alone together.

'I don't feel I have anything to prove,' she said haughtily.

'Really? You keep telling me it's not going to happen and yet twice now your body has told me different. Are you sure you can resist the temptation so easily? How do you know until you've been properly tested?'

Helen knew he was yanking her chain but to hell with him. She was feeling sufficiently goaded. 'You could give me the apple itself and I'd still be able to resist. I am in control of me.'

An image of Helen in fig leaves rose in his mind and his jeans became even more uncomfortable. He raised an eyebrow.

Helen knew this wasn't going to be over until she could prove it to him. 'What time do we leave?' she asked, returning his doubtful stare steadily.

'Just getting the picnic ready. Thirty minutes sound OK?'

She nodded. 'I'll get into my leathers and dig out my helmet.'

Leathers? She had leathers? Suddenly the fig leaves were replaced with the image of a leather-clad Helen removing her helmet and shaking her hair loose. Why did fully clothed biker-chick Helen seem more erotic than a scantily clad fig-leaf one?

It had been a while since Helen had been on a bike. Her father had last shot through town two years ago and she'd gone out with him both days. She distinctly remembered the feel of her arms around his waist, hugging into his back and yet feeling that strange blend of disconnectedness she'd always felt in his company. Her love for him as a father figure warring with years of childhood disappointments.

The exhilaration, the freedom both James and her father thrived on hit her almost immediately and she understood their addiction. To a point. It was thrilling. Stimulating. Invigorating. But not to the exclusion of all else. Not to the exclusion of life's little realities. Or inconveniences. Like a wife and child.

She spent the first ten minutes holding onto James while keeping as much space as possible between them. Her fingers clutched a handful of his leather jacket on either side while she held herself stiffly, trying to maintain some distance. But there wasn't much room on the back of a bike and it didn't take long for her body to protest the rather unnatural position she'd adopted.

James wondered how long Helen could keep the stiff posture up for. Aside from everything else she was messing up the aerodynamics. She was supposed to mould herself to his back, fit into his contours, not sit as if he'd suddenly grown spines like the echidna they'd just seen by the roadside.

'Relax,' he yelled over the engine noise and the wind rushing like a cyclone around them. 'Put your arms around me.'

Helen acquiesced, reluctantly at first, settling herself stiffly against him. But as the growling vintage engine ate up the miles she slowly relaxed, her body easing gradually until her front was in full contact with his back. Her arms crept forward until they were fully encircling his waist. It was easy then to just let all the tension go and melt against him.

James felt the moment she finally succumbed. Her weight pressed against him, her arms tightened around his waist and although he knew it wasn't possible, he thought he felt her sigh. There was something elemental about being on a bike, the sun beating down and the open road in front of you. And a woman draped around you. He smiled a contented smile.

The last twenty-five kilometres of their journey took them into a mountain range and national park. The bike slowed to negotiate the winding road and bends and the shade of towering trees allowed only dappled sunlight through the canopy. There was a bit of traffic about, too, slowing their way, people no doubt keen to visit the springs also. When they finally pulled up in the car park they'd been travelling for nearly two hours.

'That was great,' Helen enthused as she alighted and took her helmet off. She shook her head to unruffle her helmet hair.

James took his time taking his own off. She'd fulfilled all his wildest fantasies with that head shake and he didn't want his eyes betraying the fact that Eve was already tempting him with the apple.

'Yep,' he said, making a show of hanging his helmet over the handlebars. 'Nothing quite like it.'

Helen looked around. 'So, do you have a plan in mind for the day?'

James looked down as he removed his gloves, quelling the suggestion her innocent question had raised. He shrugged. 'You're the local. Is there one spot better than another?'

Helen shrugged the backpack off her shoulders and handed it to him. 'There are two major pools but there are literally hundreds of little springs around here so anywhere's good.'

James took the pack. 'Lead the way.'

Helen grinned. She was pleased he had goaded her up here. It had been a while since she'd been and she'd forgotten what a truly beautiful spot it was. With the towering eucalypts, plentiful tree ferns and numerous thermal pools it was like a little piece of heaven.

Still, she wasn't stupid enough to take him to any of the more secluded pools. She hadn't forgotten the reason why she was up here and she certainly wasn't going to give him an unfair advantage.

She followed the short track to the main pool and was satisfied to see several family groups and couples had set up camp around the edges. It wasn't crowded enough to ruin the enjoyment but it wasn't deserted either.

'This looks perfect,' she said, finding a spot not too close to anyone but near enough to be in full view.

James raised an amused eyebrow. 'You think prying eyes are going to help you keep your hands off me?'

'I don't need any help,' she replied steadily. 'They're to keep you honest.'

He chuckled. 'You think I care about an audience?'

Helen swallowed. No, he probably didn't. She ignored his comment and unzipped her jacket. 'I'm going for a swim.'

She was conscious of his gaze on her as she quickly stripped down to the black one-piece she had on beneath her leathers. She daren't even look at him when she was done, afraid of the desire she'd seen in his eyes. She just turned and plunged straight into the pool.

James stared helplessly after her. She'd pulled off her clothes and was gone in what seemed like the blink of an eye but the bit in the middle would be burned on his retinas for ever. A swimsuit that covered everything but left nothing to the imagination. The bulge of her breasts, the curve of her waist, the slimness of her shoulders and waist and the jut of her hip.

He felt a droplet of water hit his cheek and he looked down to find her splashing him. 'Come on in. It's gorgeous.'

The warmth of the water enveloped her instantly and she lay on her back as she waited for him to join her. The heat was drugging and she pondered the supposed detoxifying qualities of the springs as she stared at the little squares of blue sky just visible through the lush canopy. Local legend had it that spirits lived in the springs.

She felt water land on her face and she popped her head up in time to see him swiping his arm in a wide arc across the surface and thrusting in her direction. She couldn't see what he was wearing. All she could see was his magnificent naked chest decorated with its dainty medallion and she prayed to the spirits, if they existed, for restraint.

They wallowed in the water for an hour, chatting occasionally. Helen gave him the tourist blurb on the local area and he listened attentively. A beach ball landed between them and for twenty minutes they got caught up in an impromptu volleyball game.

'I'm starving,' Helen said as the game came to a close.

'Lets eat, then.'

Helen watched as his powerful arm muscles boosted him out of the pool. Water sluiced off his hair and down his back in a fluid sheet, his muscles flexing as he twisted. He stood and she was treading water in the pool, staring up at him.

It was a very bad vantage point. His usually tall frame looked potently dominant. His legs looked longer, his quads bulkier. His chest broader. Black Lycra briefs, similar to cyclist pants and just covering his upper thighs, moulded his hips, buttocks and the contours of his manhood.

'Here,' he said, and held out his hand to her.

Helen was too dumbfounded to refuse. She took his hand and he pulled her out of the water as if she weighed no more than a feather. She stumbled against him briefly as she found her footing but quickly stepped back and dropped her hand from his.

She found her towel and quickly dried herself off, paying particular attention to her hair. The warmth of the day would dry her skin and costume quickly. It was her thick hair that would take for ever.

James also dried off quickly and then threw the towel down on the ground and sat on it as he pulled things out of the backpack. By the time Helen had sat too he had it all prepared. Mini-quiches, ham and salad rolls stuffed with filling and a fruit platter. He'd even thrown in two long-necked beers.

'Wow, this looks amazing,' Helen said, pulling on her T-shirt. She knew she'd never have the nerve to sit in her costume as he was and not cover up.

She accepted the beer and clinked the neck against his. 'Cheers.'

They ate in silence for the most part, content to absorb their surroundings and let other people's conversation drift around them. James's medallion moved with every movement of his jaw and Helen's eyes were drawn irresistibly to it.

She reached forward and picked the delicate piece of jewellery off the broad expanse of chest. 'Is that a St Christopher?' she asked.

He nodded. 'Patron saint of travellers.'

She dropped it back against his neck. 'Did someone give it to you?'

He gave her a steady stare. 'It belonged to my father. It came with the bike.'

She was surprised. It was so fine, almost feminine she'd assumed that a woman had given it to him. Of course, it looked curiously at home around the corded muscles of his neck. On any other man it may have even looked effeminate but he was so masculine it just looked…right.

Helen took a long swallow of her beer, her eyes focused on the St Christopher, not daring to look lower. 'Tell me about your dad.'

James drained the contents of his bottle. 'Not much to tell.' He shrugged. 'He married my mother because she was pregnant with me. He stayed until the day I left for uni and then he took off.'

He was tense. She could see the muscles of his shoulders and neck were corded tight, the veins protruded, a pulse hammered in the hollow of his throat. 'They weren't happy.'

He gave a harsh laugh. 'Now, there's an understatement! I don't remember a time when they were ever happy.'

Helen could hear the bitterness in his voice. 'They argued a lot?'

James shook his head. 'No. They didn't. No more than any other couple, I guess. They just co-existed. They got married through some twisted sense of obligation to me and then felt trapped by it for the rest of their lives. They were very different people, who didn't really get on. The only thing they shared in common was me. They were polite but distant. Not very demonstrative or emotional.'

Helen drew her knees up and rested her chin on them. Her heart bled for him. His childhood sounded so desolate. At least she'd had Elsie's love and care. At least she'd felt wanted by someone. His turquoise gaze stared past her. He hadn't looked her in the eye since the conversation had begun. 'It sounds lonely.'

'It was,' he said abruptly. He really didn't want to spoil this time with her by dredging up his past.

'I'm sorry, I'm prying. You don't want to talk about this.'

James looked at her then. He saw the compassion warming the amber flecks in her cool jade eyes. He sighed. 'No, it's OK. It doesn't matter. It's…a long time ago now.'

But living in Skye, being embraced by the community, seeing Helen with Elsie, had bought his childhood back into sharp focus. He'd thought about those days a lot recently. Skye's easy acceptance of him had made him acutely aware of what he'd missed out on.

'Families are…complicated,' she agreed.

James nodded. He started to peel the label off his beer bottle. 'I always got the sense that I was in the way of the lives they wanted to lead. Like I was a nuisance. Don't get me wrong. They didn't beat me or anything.'

'They just neglected you emotionally.' The thought of a little boy wandering around a house, aching for someone to pay him a little attention, was awful.

James heard the sharpness of her tone as he pulled at the label. 'No. Not on purpose. They just were too caught up in their own sadness to notice I was there most of the time.'

James dropped the denuded bottle down on the ground beside him and started peeling the label off hers. The St Christopher swung gently with his movements.

'I'm sorry,' she said.

'Hey, its OK. I turned out all right.' He grinned.

She looked at his self-deprecating smile and he looked completely unaffected. Except that shadow in his eyes that she'd seen lurking that first day was suddenly explained. Sure, he seemed fine, but he travelled from place to place, looking for something that not even he could figure out. She knew how devastating parental behaviour could be. How a sense of family, or lack of it, isolated kids in a way that touched every aspect of their lives. For ever. No matter how grown-up they'd become.

'No thanks to your folks,' she said.

James dropped the second stripped bottle to the ground and it clanked against the first. 'They did the best they could with what they had.'

She nodded. She guessed everyone had different standards. But sharing his childhood with him had brought back her own painful memories. She could see the lost, lonely little boy and could totally relate to him. How often had she felt abandoned? How desperately had she craved being part of a real family? Was it right that children had to suffer because they were powerless and some adults made bad decisions?

Helen didn't realise how engrossed they were in their conversation until a shrill desperate plea broke the air of quiet relaxation around the pool.

'Help! Help! Is there a doctor or midwife anywhere?'

James and Helen looked up instantly at the cry for help. The panicked voice was coming from one of the many walking tracks that led from the main pool.

'Don?' Helen gasped, staring as a man and a woman came into view. She was on her feet in two seconds, followed closely by James, their wretched childhoods forgotten.

'Genevieve!' Helen exclaimed, closing the distance as she pushed through the curious crowd that had leapt to their feet at the first sign of crisis.

'Helen! James! Thank God!' Genevieve said, sagging against Helen instantly.

Helen looked into Genevieve's flushed face, her heavily pregnant abdomen looking cumbersome. 'What's wrong?' she demanded.

'I'm in labour,' Genevieve panted, clutching Helen's arm like she'd just been offered the last seat in the last lifeboat to leave the *Titanic*.

'You're ten days overdue, Genevieve, what the hell are you doing all the way out here?' Helen demanded as she glared at Don, a well-known local bushwalker.

The contraction passed and Genevieve looked at her with apprehension in her eyes. 'I was going stir crazy in the house. I had to do something to give the baby a prod. I thought a vigorous walk would stir things along. Oh…' she wailed and clutched at Don's sleeve as another pain swept through her. 'I need to push…' She doubled over.

Helen and James looked at each other. Such a definite statement from a first-time mother was alarming.

'I told her I didn't think it was wise to come so far away,' Don said, visibly paling at his wife's distress. He looked as petrified as some of the wood in the nearby forest. As a botanist, he didn't cope well with human conditions.

'When did the contractions start?' James asked, as a bystander offered them their picnic blanket and Helen helped her friend to the ground.

'Call the ambulance,' Helen said, looking blindly around and hoping someone in the crowd responded. She had a bad feeling this baby wasn't going to wait. She had a worse feeling that help would be at least an hour away. If the baby did come and there were complications, Genevieve's baby didn't stand a chance.

'We were only half an hour into our walk,' Don said, answering for his wife who was bellowing through another contraction.

'Oh, God! It's coming!' Genevieve yelled. 'I have to push.'

James looked at Helen. This was bad.

'Have a look,' James said to her out the corner of his mouth.

He threw a towel over Genevieve's drawn-up knees. 'Do you think we can have some privacy, folks?' James asked the gathering crowd, and was relieved when they broke away, even though every eye at the rock pool was still trained on them.

Helen helped Genevieve off with her shorts and undies and took a quick peek beneath the towel. The baby's head was right there.

'She's crowned,' Helen told James in a low voice.

'How may babies have you delivered?'

Helen shrugged. 'Hundreds.'

OK. There was no time to transport Genevieve to the hospital and he was with a professional who easily out-delivered him. 'Looks like this baby has its daddy's genes and wants to be born among vegetation,' James said to a panting Genevieve. 'The head's ready to deliver. Do you trust us?'

Genevieve looked from one to the other. 'Yes.'

'OK, then.' James smiled. 'Push with the next contraction. Helen's going to catch.'

'What? No. I can't believe this is happening,' Don said, looking at Helen and James in disbelief. 'We have to get her to hospital.'

Helen took up position at the business end. 'No time, Don. You're about to meet your baby.'

And in three pushes William Redmond Jacobs, all ten

pounds of him, was born, bawling and furious at the world. His lusty cries split the suddenly eerily quiet air around the rock pool. There was a collective sigh and then a burst of applause.

Helen caught him expertly and, satisfied with his condition, handed him immediately into the waiting arms of his impatient mother and father. Someone from the crowd handed Helen a clean dry towel and they covered the squawking newborn.

James squeezed her hand and they smiled at each other as they watched Genevieve and Don stare in utter amazement at the perfectness of their son. The new parents were utterly entranced.

James and Helen knew this was one child who was never going to feel unwanted.

CHAPTER SEVEN

GENEVIEVE'S baby took over the rest of the afternoon and, needless to say, they got through the day without ravishing each other. Helen accompanied the new mum as Don drove them back to Skye and James rode back alone, resigned to the fact it wasn't going to happen between him and Helen. Helen was gaga over the baby and he knew she deserved someone better at the whole family thing than him.

He remembered her saying she wanted children and he knew he couldn't do that. Maybe someone like Tom could. Maybe someone else. But he knew one thing for sure, he didn't know a damn thing about raising a happy child and he sure as hell had no plans to try.

Weeks passed and they returned to their roles as flatmates with reasonable ease. The attraction he felt for her didn't go away and he was damn sure it hadn't evaporated for her either. Sometimes he caught her looking at him and there was such raw hunger in her jade eyes it took his breath away.

But she, as promised, never once acted on it. Never even

looked like she was wavering. 'I'm an adult.' That's what she'd said and she had well and truly proved it. It was actually a good exercise for him in self-control. He'd never been in a situation before where he'd had to keep his libido in check. Pretty much any attraction he'd ever felt had been returned and well and truly acted on. Helen's don't-even-go-there aura was good practice for him should he ever be insane enough to hanker after someone else who could withstand his considerable charm.

Consequently he did a lot of exploring over the next six weeks. He went away on his bike each weekend, discovering a different part of the local area. He usually took his swag and camped out under the stars, returning on Sunday evening in time for the regular trivia night.

That just left the weekdays and nights to deal with. Thankfully work was always busy so although he saw a lot of her, it was impersonal with no time for exchanging longing looks. Nights were the most challenging. But curiously also the most rewarding. Even though it was torturous being near her and not being able to touch her, he loved her company.

She was smart and funny and they'd read a lot of the same books and had the same taste in television. She was a veritable fount of information on the local area and helped him plan his jaunts. They both loved to cook and there was something very fulfilling about hanging out in the kitchen with her, drinking wine and cooking a meal.

Before he knew it he'd been in Skye for three months. The agency he was with had been scouting out locum jobs further north and had secured him another four-month position in central Queensland. His leg was fully recovered and as hard as it was going to be to leave, he doubted he could stay any longer and not make a play for Helen. Only one month to go and it couldn't come soon enough.

'Your next patient is here, James.'

Helen's voice on the intercom stroked over his skin as vividly as the day she had touched his leg newly released from its fibreglass prison. He groaned inwardly. Every day of the next month was going to be hell.

'Send him in.'

He greeted Val and Joshua as they walked through his door a few seconds later and shut the door after them.

James looked at the little blond-haired, blue-eyed boy that he'd saved from drowning. He looked none the worse for it. He had a really mischievous glint in his eyes and James had heard all about what a handful the lad was.

He grinned at the boy. 'Joshua, my man, what have you been up to this time?'

'I have a 'sistent sniffle.'

James noted the stream of clear mucus running from the boys left nostril and laughed. 'That sounds bad.'

'Persistent,' Val said apologetically, pulling out a tissue and wiping her uncooperative son's nose.

Val looked stressed and tired. Exasperated. 'How long has he had it?' James asked, opening Josh's substantial chart.

Val's brow furrowed. 'About a week. But it's really strange. It's just one side. He hasn't had a fever or a cough or even felt unwell. He's been haring around at a million miles an hour into everything as usual.'

James watched Josh as he ran a grubby-looking toy car along the edge of the desk, making brm noises.

'His left eye is really watery all the time, too,' Val continued. 'I thought it was a cold and would go away, but now I'm not so sure. Maybe it's an allergy.'

'Is he allergic to anything?' James asked, flipping though the notes. Josh had produced another car and was crashing the two together, making smashing noises now.

'No.'

'Any itching or welts or rashes?'

'No.'

He nodded. 'Come on, then, Josh, climb up on my bench over there and I'll have a look at your sniffle.'

Josh picked up his cars and followed James over. He placed the cars on the examination couch as he stepped on the footstool and climbed onto the bed.

James took a moment to look at his young patient. He noted the exudate collecting in the corner of Josh's left eye and listened carefully to the boy's breathing. He put his finger against Josh's right nostril. 'Big breath in, Josh.'

Josh puffed up his chest and James noted that the inhalation seemed a little obstructed. 'Again,' he said.

Josh repeated the action and James was even more convinced there was some kind of blockage in his nose. He pulled a penlight out of his pocket, tilted Josh's head back and directed the beam of light into the left nostril. He thought he could see an odd fleck of blue right at the back.

'Josh, I'm going to keep my finger on this nostril and I want you to blow really hard through the other one, OK? Just like you're blowing your nose.'

The boy nodded and blew. Nothing. 'Again,' James said. 'Really hard.' Still nothing. He shone the light up again but whatever the blue fleck was, it hadn't budged.

'Well, Val,' James said. 'I think there may be a foreign body up there. Something irritating the mucous membrane and obstructing the left side of his nose.'

'Oh, no.' Val leapt to her feet. 'Josh, did you put something up your nose?' she asked.

Josh looked at his mother and James could see the sudden look of wariness on his face. He knew he was in trouble. He shook his head but it was plain that Josh wasn't telling the truth.

'What are we going to do?'

James could see the worry and gathering tears on the mother's face. 'It's OK, Val. I'll have a go at pulling it out. If I can grasp it easily, it should be OK. But if it's hard to remove we don't want to push it further into his airway so he'll need an X-ray and maybe he'll need to have it removed under general anaesthetic.'

'Oh, God,' said Val.

'It's OK.' James took a moment to reassure her. 'That's the worst-case scenario.'

Val nodded and James hit the intercom. 'Helen, could I see you for a moment, please?'

Four weeks, Helen thought. Only four more weeks of her stomach doing that silly loopy thing every time his voice purred into her ear.

'You called?' she said as she opened the door.

'Josh appears to have a foreign body up his nose. Do we keep some long-nosed forceps for this kind of extraction?'

'Joshua Lutton,' Helen said, shaking her head at the guilty-looking child. 'Boys, huh?' she said to Val.

'Hey!' James protested.

Val laughed. 'Katrina never did anything like this.'

Helen laughed, too. 'Hang tight. I'll be back in a jiffy.'

Helen returned a couple of minutes later with sterile packaged forceps. 'Do you need a hand?'

'Maybe just to hold him.'

Helen nodded. 'OK, then, come on, Josh. Lie back on the pillow. This won't take a moment.' The child looked at her apprehensively and seemed as if he was about to cry. 'Mummy's going to be here, holding your hand, aren't you, Mummy?'

Val dabbed at her eyes. 'Yes,' she said, smiling at her son as she took his hand.

James undid the packaging and positioned himself near Josh's head. 'You ready?' he said to Helen.

She nodded. 'OK, Josh, we need you to be very still and very brave now.'

'That shouldn't be hard,' James said to Helen. 'I heard Josh Lutton is the bravest kid in Skye.'

'That's right.' Helen smiled at James. 'Isn't that right, Josh?'

Josh's wobbling chin smoothed out and he nodded bravely. 'That's what Grandpa Alf says,' he agreed in a little voice as the three adults loomed over him.

'He's a very wise man is your grandpa,' James agreed. 'All righty, then, Helen's going to tilt your head up and I'm going to pull whatever's up there out. On three. Ready? One.'

James advanced the small metal forceps to sit just outside the nose entrance. Helen held the penlight in one hand and the patient's head in the other. She shone it up Josh's nostril as she held him securely.

'Two.' James inserted the forceps gently. Josh flinched a little and Helen increased the pressure on the boy's forehead, but he stayed still.

'Three.' He opened the forceps and made a grab for the fleck of blue he could see. The forceps scraped against something hard and he manoeuvred them gently to grasp it, hoping he wouldn't push the object further into the airway and possibly block it altogether.

'Got it,' he said, breathing out as he slowly withdrew the forceps. He had no idea how big the object was or if it had any sharp edges that could cause damage on the way out, so he took his time to remove it gently.

James bought the object out into the open and held it up to the light. It was a small, white, hard, plastic figure in a sitting position with blue feet.

Val gasped. 'It's from one of his toy cars,' she said.

Helen released her hold on Josh and he sat up. Val grabbed him and hugged him. 'Never, ever put anything up your nose, Joshy. Never. Do you hear me?' She gave her son a gentle shake.

'It seems like we are constantly in debt to you, Dr Remington,' Val said, turning to him as she rocked a bewildered Josh in her arms.

James shrugged. 'Nonsense. It's my job and boys are natural explorers. Let me just have another look up to make sure he didn't decide to put another one up there in case that one got lonely.'

James shone his torch up again and was satisfied he couldn't see anything more. He asked Josh to breathe again through one nostril and was pleased to hear that it no longer sounded obstructed.

'Thanks again, Dr Remington. He's a gem, that one, Helen,' Val said to her as she gathered Josh to go.

'Yes,' Helen said, conscious of James's amused gaze.

'Are you sure you can't stay? Skye's going to miss you. I don't think Josh will want to see anyone else ever again.'

Helen turned and raised an eyebrow at him. 'James isn't a stayer,' she said dryly.

He ignored her. 'I'm sorry, Val. I've already said yes to another locum job up north. I start in five weeks.'

Helen wasn't prepared for that piece of news. She pulled the white sheet off the examination table to hide the squall of emotions that lashed her insides. He really was leaving. He hadn't even checked to see if they wanted him for longer in case Genevieve changed her mind about coming back so early after the baby's birth. He'd obviously stayed as long as he was going to in Skye.

'Our loss,' Val said. 'Say goodbye to Dr Remington, Josh.'

'Knowing Josh, we should maybe just say see you later.' James smiled.

Val laughed. 'Believe me sincerely when I say this, Dr Remington. I like you. A lot. But I hope Josh never has to see you in a medical context ever again.'

'Fair enough.' James grinned and waved at Josh as they walked out the door.

They watched the empty doorway for a few seconds. 'Where up north?' she asked.

He turned to face her. 'The gemfields.'

She nodded. 'It's nice around there.' She looked down at the sheet bundled up in her arms. 'I'll send your next patient in.'

James watched her go. *It was pretty nice around here, too.*

* * *

A week later the telephone rang at two a.m. Helen, who had only fallen asleep twenty minutes before and was consequently deep in the land of nod, didn't even hear it. It wasn't until James knocked on her door that she pulled herself out of the sticky bonds of slumber.

'What?' she called, completely disorientated for a few seconds.

'The phone's for you. It's Duncan.'

It took a few more seconds for her to wake up properly. She flew out of bed and nearly ran straight into James as she pulled the door open and raced to the phone.

'Hello?'

James stood nearby as Helen took the call. A phone call in the middle of the night could not be good. He watched her face. Her loose hair fell forward and obscured it as she said 'Uhuh' and 'Yep' and shook her head a lot.

Helen replaced the receiver. 'Elsie's been rushed to hospital. They found her unconscious half an hour ago. She was in cardiac arrest. They think she's had a massive heart attack.'

'Oh, Helen,' he said, moving towards her, 'I'm so sorry.'

She looked at him. 'Duncan said Jonathon doesn't think she'll recover.'

He moved closer and held out his arms. He was wearing boxers and a tight T-shirt and his chest looked so cosy, so right, but she daren't succumb to its lure.

'No,' she said, slipping past him. 'I'm OK. I just have to get there.'

When Helen came out of the bedroom James was dressed in jeans and a T-shirt, waiting for her. She stopped short. 'Go to bed, James,' she said. 'You don't have to come with me.'

James shook his head. 'I know. But what kind of human being would I be if I let you go alone? Come on, I'll drive you.'

Helen opened her mouth to argue. She didn't need his help. She was used to doing things alone. She'd been dealing with things alone for all her life. It would be dangerous to get used to having him around. To depend on him.

If only the ache in her arms, in her heart would go away. The need to be held for once, to lean on someone at this moment, was almost unbearable. She'd known this day would come eventually but now it was here her courage was deserting her.

'Helen?'

His voice was soft, his turquoise gaze compassionate, and for a moment her composure teetered. But she snatched it back at the last second, acquiescing with a brisk nod, not trusting her voice.

They drove in silence and were at their destination in under ten minutes. He followed her in and Helen didn't protest. She realised two things. One, she was scared. Scared of what she was about to see. And, two, she didn't want to be alone.

'Hi, Helen,' the night nurse greeted her, and filled her in on Elsie's condition. 'She's in the HDU.' The high dependency unit. Things were serious.

Helen nodded and made her way there. Duncan embraced her, his worried face speaking volumes. She stood at the end of Elsie's bed, the only thing visible from her vantage point was sparse white hair. She was too frightened to get closer.

James could sense Helen was only just holding it all together. She was standing so rigidly not even her ponytail moved. Her hand gripped the bed end with white-knuckled intensity. She looked so isolated, so remote it was painful to watch. He desperately wanted to touch her, pull her into his arms, but he'd never seen her look more untouchable. He doubted she would welcome it.

Instead, he pulled up a chair for her. 'Sit,' he said to her gently, touching her arm to bring her out of her almost trance-like state. She looked at him blankly and he pointed to the chair he'd placed next to Duncan's, on the side Elsie was facing.

'Th-thanks,' Helen said, her legs responding automatically to his command.

Helen sank into the chair slowly. She could see Elsie fully now and her appearance was deeply shocking. She looked like a shadow of herself, a shadow of the woman she'd seen only yesterday. She looked almost unrecognisable.

Helen pulled the lever on the bedframe near her knees and collapsed the side rail that was barricading Elsie from them. She touched her hand tentatively, the sensation evoking a hundred memories.

Suddenly she wanted to be closer. She wanted to crawl into bed beside her, like she had as a little girl. She wanted to hear Elsie's smooth voice singing to her, cuddling her, telling her everything was going to be fine.

She felt hot tears well in her eyes and spill down her cheeks. The one person who'd given her the one thing her childish heart had craved more than anything—a sense of family—was fading away. She dashed them away.

She wouldn't cry. Elsie didn't approve of tears. Elsie believed that when your time was up it was up, and particularly since the stroke she'd known she'd been living on borrowed time. And one look at an utterly devastated Duncan told her she had to be strong for this last part. She grabbed her surrogate brother's hand and gave it a squeeze.

Absurdly, she wished her father was there. Just for once she wished he was there for her. She glanced at James. He was here. Ironic that the one man that was here for her was as much of a gypsy as her father. A man cut from the same cloth. He was here now and she was grateful but in a few weeks he'd get on his Harley and disappear. She'd never felt lonely before. Not ever. Until tonight.

'Hello, Elsie. It's Helen. Duncan and I are here. We're right here. We're not going anywhere.'

Nothing. Elsie's breath misted the inside of the oxygen mask that covered her face. What had she expected? For Elsie to open her eyes and smile at her? Make a last-ditch crack at getting her and James together? She stroked the aged hand, the papery skin, the prominent bones. An IV taped securely into the crook of Elsie's elbow dripped a steady supply of sugary saline into her system to keep her hydrated. A monitor blipped in the background and Helen was alarmed at the frequency of ectopic beats.

She looked at James over her mother's head. He was sitting on the opposite side of the bed, yawning, feigning interest in a two-year-old woman's magazine. 'You should go. You don't need to hang around.'

He shrugged. 'I don't mind.'

'It's not necessary.' Their gazes locked. 'Duncan's here.'

Duncan looked incapable of any higher functions. He looked absolutely gutted. 'I'll stay another hour or so.'

Helen didn't have the inclination to argue with him. It somehow didn't seem peculiar that someone who had been a complete stranger to her three months ago was sitting with her while the woman who had been more of a mother to her than her own mother slowly let go of life. Oddly enough, it seemed kind of right.

Helen shuffled her chair closer to the bed and laid her head on the mattress close to her Elsie's face. It was wrinkled and gaunt, her eyes sunken, her mouth minus her dentures sucked in, her lips thin and dry. This wasn't Elsie. Helen cradled a bony hand against her face and shut her eyes, letting memories of her childhood wash over her.

An hour later the small magazine print started to blur and James's eyes lost the battle to stay open. As he slipped into slumber his neck slowly lost its ability to hold his head up. It nodded forward and he woke with a start, snapping his head back up.

His eyes slowly came back into focus and he rubbed at the crick in his neck. Duncan had nodded off in his chair. Helen appeared to have fallen asleep also, her head resting on the mattress. He stood and stretched, the hard plastic chair not the most comfortable piece of furniture he'd ever sat on.

The air-conditioning was quite cool and he wandered out to the nurses' station and asked for a blanket. They furnished him with one and he placed it gently over Helen's shoulders. She murmured something unintelligible and snuggled into the folds.

Elsie's breath still misted the mask and, along with the monitor noise, James knew she was still with them. For now anyway. James had read Elsie's chart and she appeared to have had an extended down time. At her age, and with her history, her care was purely palliative. He took his seat again.

A nurse came by every half an hour and checked on their patient. One of them bought him a steaming-hot coffee at one stage and he sipped it gratefully. It had been a long time since he had maintained a bedside vigil and he'd forgotten how much caffeine helped. Even bad-tasting caffeine.

The day dawned, soft light blanketing the landscape. The sun rose, pushing the velvety glow aside, streaming in through the windows, its brightness an early warning of another hot day.

Two nurses came in to shift Elsie's position. They shook Helen gently and she stirred, her eyes opening to see the reassuring misting of the face mask.

She sat up slowly and rubbed at her neck. Her bleary-eyed gaze fell on a yawning James. He'd been there all night? 'You stayed,' she murmured, as she moved out of the way.

'Yes.'

The slow smile he gave her banished the tired lines around his eyes and she felt stupidly happy. 'You shouldn't have. You've got to work today.'

He shrugged. 'I'm a doctor. I'm no stranger to all-nighters.'

Helen yawned. 'What's the time?'

'Six. Let's get a coffee while they do this,' he suggested.

Helen saw Duncan off—he needed to duck home for a few hours—and then joined James in the lounge area. She stared out the window while he made her a drink.

'Here. I'm sorry, it's just that horrible instant stuff.'

He nudged her shoulder and she turned away from the view of Main Street, accepting the cup. They sipped in silence for a while.

'I have to make some phone calls,' Helen said. 'I need to arrange for Donna to take over at the surgery.'

James nodded. Donna was a local mother who worked as a part-time receptionist when Helen manned the extra clinics the surgery ran.

'Will she be able to at such short notice?'

'I hope so,' Helen said. 'Given the circumstances, I'm sure she won't mind. It won't be for long.' Helen stood as the import of her words hit her. Elsie was dying. This really was the end.

James watched as she paced to the window and felt completely helpless. She was standing rigidly again, looking so very, very alone.

'I have to ring my father, too. He'll want to know.'

'Where is he at the moment? Will it take him long to get here?' James felt certain that Elsie's death was reasonably imminent. Helen may not look like she needed anyone but surely her father should be there.

'I have no idea where he is. Or if he'll make it in time. I just have a number of a service to ring. He checks it every now and then.'

James nodded. Her voice was curiously lacking in emotion. She'd obviously learnt a long time ago to never get her hopes up where her father was concerned. It seemed so sad in the current circumstances to not be able to lean on the one other person who had given you life.

'How often do you see him?'

Helen shrugged and turned back to face him. 'The last time was two years ago.'

She sounded matter-of-fact. 'You sound very tolerant of him.'

'I guess Elsie had a big influence on me there. She always encouraged me to have a relationship with him. To accept him for what he was. Accept his transience and that the time we had together was finite. She understood he didn't know how to cope with Mum, or with me, and I guess in lots of ways she made excuses for him because I was a child struggling to understand my mother's illness and I didn't need to deal with my father's shortcomings as well. And I guess I bought it.'

'You were a child. He was your father. Of course you wanted to look up to him.' He understood that better than anyone.

'And I did. But as much as I love him, there are times when I've felt really neglected by him.' *Like right now.*

'I'm sorry,' he said. It seemed like they'd both been abandoned by the people who should have been looking out for them.

They stared at each other for a few moments, united in the solidarity of a similar background. The nurse who had been tending to Elsie's pressure-area care bustled into the lounge, breaking their connection. 'We're finished,' she announced. 'You can go back in if you like.'

Helen gulped down the rest of the contents of her mug.

'Go now,' she said to him. 'You need to get ready for work. I'll just make these phone calls then I'll head back in.'

James hesitated. 'Are you sure? I don't like leaving you alone.'

She smiled. 'I know every person in this hospital, James. Heavens, I know everyone in Skye. I'm not alone.'

Still he hesitated. 'I'll pop by at lunchtime. Ring me if…if you need me before that.'

Helen watched him leave. She called to him as he reached the open doorway of the lounge and he turned back. 'Thank you,' she murmured.

He nodded and left.

Elsie died the following day at lunchtime. She'd started Cheyne-Stokes breathing that morning and Helen had known it was close. Every laboured breath Elsie had taken had teetered on the edge of her last, the pause between each respiration stretching interminably. James had been by her side when the next breath hadn't come.

Helen didn't cry, just held Elsie's hand tight and stroked her hair as she comforted a sobbing Denise and a dazed Duncan. James left to give the family some privacy, returning a few hours later after a concerned phone call from one of the nurses.

Helen sat there, her face blank, her hand stroking Elsie's. James touched her shoulder lightly and she shrugged it off. 'I'm fine,' she said, her breath frozen inside her, along with a huge block of emotions. 'I'm fine.'

James sat with her until Helen was ready to let go. He took her elbow and guided her up out of the chair, concerned by her lack of emotion.

She pulled away. 'I'm fine,' she insisted. 'Go back to work. I've got a funeral to organise.'

She left and he watched her go, looking untouchable in her grief.

In control.

Fine.

Except he wasn't buying it. Not for a moment.

CHAPTER EIGHT

HELEN continued to be 'fine' for the next week. They delayed the funeral as long as possible in the hope that her father would be able to make it in time. Elsie had understood Owen better than anyone, had never been judgmental about him, and Helen knew her father would want to be there.

She hadn't heard from him but then she hadn't expected to either. Her father had a habit of just turning up. But the funeral couldn't be delayed inevitably and a week after she died Elsie was scheduled to be buried.

Owen Franklin knocked on Helen's door the morning of the funeral. James opened it and knew who it was instantly. The tall man in leathers didn't seem to have aged any from the photo that stood on the coffee-table. His hair was greyer but there was a vitality about him that belied his years. He smiled, revealing perfect white teeth, and shook James's hand, exuding charisma.

'I'm pleased you got here in time. Helen will be most relieved.'

'Yes, I have cut it a bit fine, haven't I?' Owen remarked as he wandered around the lounge room, inspecting things. 'I was in Broome—only found out a few days ago.'

What? No telephones in Broome? James wasn't impressed by Owen's cavalier attitude and felt a curious urge to give him a piece of his mind. He'd been going out of his mind, worrying about Helen's emotional state. Her insistence on being fine, her stoic refusal to grieve.

Hell, she'd been back at work the next day and no amount of persuasion or bullying by him or Frank had swayed her. Would it have killed her father to ring, to reach out to his daughter? Just once?

'What time is the funeral?'

'Eleven.'

Owen nodded. 'Is my girl around?'

'She's in the shower. I'll let her know you're here.'

Owen put a hand on James's shoulder as he passed. 'Are you and Helen…involved?'

What? The man was going to get all proprietorial now? All fatherly? James felt his hackles rise and he stared pointedly at Owen's hand until the older man dropped it. *No, I'm just the one who's been here for her.*

'No. I'm just the locum. Helen's been putting up with me for a few months.'

Helen heard her father's query and James's denial as she walked down the hallway. She remembered the heat of his mouth and, despite knowing it was for the best, his quick dismissal hit her like an arrow to the solar plexus. Had she truly expected anything different?

When she entered the lounge the two men were sizing each other up. 'Hi, Dad.'

Owen opened his arms and Helen went straight to him. 'You made it,' she said, her words muffled as she pressed her face into his chest. She inhaled his familiar aftershave and leaned into him. God, she'd missed him.

'I'm sorry I couldn't get here any sooner.'

Helen pulled back, heard the gruffness in his voice, and knew in his own way that this was affecting him. 'It's OK. You're here now.'

'That's the girl, chin up. Elsie was a tough old bird who lived a great life. She wouldn't have wanted any of us to shed tears over her passing.'

James watched Helen nod, dry-eyed, and despaired. *Chin up?* He had hoped her father's arrival would be the key to unlocking Helen's fettered emotions. That she would see him and all the emotions she'd stored up would be released and she'd burst into tears. But if he was going to give her the chin-up routine…

'Here, I got you this.' Owen pulled a small white packet out of his pocket.

Helen took the offering from him, noticing the dimple in his chin, so like James's. She opened it and peered inside. 'Oh, Dad, it's beautiful,' she said. A small white mother-of-pearl duck lay nestled in some tissue paper.

Owen grinned. 'I thought you'd like it. Got it in Broome.'

Helen ran her fingers over the smooth, milky contours. 'Thanks,' she said, pecking her father on the cheek. She placed it on the shelf with the others and admired it. Her father had brought her most of them from his travels.

'Come on, I bet you've been driving all night and haven't even eaten yet.' She smiled at her father, pleased beyond words that he was there. The only other person in the world who truly understood how much Elsie had meant to her. 'I'll cook you some breakfast.'

'Ah, you know me so well.' Owen chuckled.

James watched them leave the room, hands linked. He marvelled at how close they seemed, given how little Owen had been around. OK, Helen hadn't dissolved into tears as he had hoped, but her body looked more relaxed, her face less taut, her shoulders less tense, the amber flecks glowing warmly in her eyes again instead of the vacant jade chill that had been there for the last ten days.

Her genuine smile had spoken a thousand words. Relief and gratitude and love. She seemed sincerely touched by her father's gift and accepted his presence with no form of censure. He could hear their chatter floating out from the kitchen and it sounded familiar, intimate. As he slipped out of the house James hoped that, whatever their interaction, Helen got what she really needed from her father to help her get through her loss. Not just a lousy duck.

James passed Owen's bike in the drive as he walked the short distance to the surgery. Had he not been so annoyed with the man, James would have stopped and admired the gleaming chrome of the powerful Harley. But for the life of him he couldn't understand what would possess a father to abandon his ill wife and child, and the chrome instantly lost all its shine. His cold, lonely childhood suddenly looked rosy by comparison.

The surgery stayed open until ten-thirty. All the patients that morning commented on Owen Franklin rolling back into town and all had an opinion on his lifestyle. Most were disparaging about it, puzzled by it even, although all agreed he was a difficult man to dislike. And their loyalty to Helen demanded at least a grudging acceptance of him.

James tried not to get involved, his own quickly formed opinion a lot less charitable. He was relieved when they shut their doors and he could have respite from the pros and cons of Owen Franklin. He felt nervous about the approaching funeral, worried about Helen's continuing emotional void and unsure of his place. He wanted to be by Helen's side as he had been since Elsie's death but she didn't need him now her father had returned.

He snorted to himself as he grabbed the jacket he'd brought to work with him that morning. Who was he kidding? She hadn't needed him anyway, with or without Owen. Every person in Skye had been around, comforting her, feeding her, worrying about her. Had she wanted it, any one of them would have lent her their shoulders to cry on, their arms to hold her. No, sirree, she didn't need him at all.

Still, James hesitated as he stepped out of the surgery. Should he call in at the cottage and see if she wanted him to escort her? He wanted to—badly. He'd become quite protective of her these days and the urge to seek her out, check how she was doing was very strong. But she needed this time with her father. To reconnect. To reminisce. She didn't need a third wheel.

It was eerie, walking through Skye. All the businesses were either shut or in the process of shutting down as he passed. Everyone in the town would be at the funeral and most appeared to be there already as he approached the church. The churchyard was almost full. Clusters of people, chatting in low voices, waited for the hearse to arrive.

He nodded to each group as he passed, amazed at the fact that he seemed to know everyone after a few short months. He made his way over to Don and Genevieve, who were standing with Frank.

'How's she doing this morning?' Genevieve asked, bouncing an almost two-month-old William on her hip.

James held out his finger and the baby gave him a dribbly smile as he reached out and clasped it. 'The same.'

Genevieve tut-tutted. 'So she's still fine?'

He nodded. 'Her father arrived just before eight, so I'm hoping she'll have vented with him.'

'Doesn't look like it,' Frank said, indicating with a nod of his head.

James turned and saw Helen and her father walking into the churchyard with the rest of Elsie's family who'd travelled to Skye for the funeral. Helen had her arm around a sobbing Denise. She was dressed in a simple black dress, her hair pulled back in its usual ponytail. She looked a little more relaxed but Frank was right, she didn't look like she'd spent the last few hours sobbing her heart out. She smiled at everyone as she made her way into the church and even stopped to comfort a couple of obviously upset people.

The hearse pulled up, the flower-draped coffin visible through the glass.

'I gotta go,' Frank said. 'Duty calls.' He was one of the pallbearers.

The milling crowd slowly trooped inside. James sat with Genevieve and Don three seats from the front. He could see Helen's erect frame easily, her ponytail brushing the nape of her neck, her father's arm firmly around her shoulders. There was nothing about her stature that indicated she would break down and cry. And it seemed an awful thing to be hoping for but if anyone needed a good howl it was Helen.

Helen went through the motions at the funeral. Sang when the organ played, bowed her head when the minister prayed, even said 'Amen' in the right places. There were some lovely tributes and it was impossible to stop the hot tears that stung at her eyes, demanding release.

But every time a well of emotion rose in her chest she took some deep calming breaths and blinked hard. Her father was right. Elsie wouldn't want any of them to mourn her passing. She would not cry.

The service came to an end and Helen rose, her legs shaking as she watched the coffin being carried out of the church. She put her arm around Duncan as he led the procession outside to the graveyard. She caught James's eye as she passed his pew and saw the concern in his eyes.

He'd been a wonderful support this last week. He'd been largely silent but always there. Making sure she ate, checking on her frequently and screening the number of visitors. She knew he was worried about her lack of emotion, had tried to speak to her about it on a couple of occasions, but he hadn't pushed and had backed off when she had asked him to.

The truth was she couldn't let herself go in front of him. That would take their strange mustn't-cross-the-line relationship to a new level and that was too painful to contemplate with someone who was going to be gone in a few short weeks. She had lain in bed every night feeling so desolate, so alone, craving his embrace but knowing that it wouldn't help. Knowing that she'd just want more.

The ceremony continued at the graveside and her father took her hand. She drew strength from his solidness. Physically and emotionally. She felt the love and support of the entire town surrounding her, and as the coffin was lowered her father squeezed her hand and she squeezed back.

The wake was held in the CWA hall. James didn't stick around for long. The surgery was scheduled to open again at one and he had volunteered to man it, including the reception desk, so everyone else could attend the wake. Helen was surrounded by a constantly changing crowd of locals, all hugging her and passing on their condolences.

James was relieved to see Owen sticking close, his arm around his daughter's waist, being attentive and supportive. Good. If ever there was a time she needed her old man it was now. He hoped she'd lean on him hard for these next few days and find a way to grieve for what she had lost. Owen Franklin certainly owed his daughter that.

It was a slow afternoon with only a trickle of patients. Most people had progressed from the wake to the pub. Very few businesses had reopened. The agency had faxed him a copy of the contract for the next locum job and he read it thoroughly between patients, deciding to sign it later. It was going to be strange, leaving Skye. For the first time in his life he felt like he belonged to a family. The connections he'd made here were strong and walking away would be harder than he'd ever imagined possible.

James didn't go back to the house when he shut up shop for the day. He wasn't sure where Helen and her father had ended up but he wanted to give them some privacy. So he headed for the pub. It was very crowded tonight, many of the funeral attendees still hanging around.

He sat with Alf and a couple of other old-timers as they reminisced about Elsie. They drank cold beer and ate thick steaks. A footy game was showing on the big-screen television.

'Wonderful woman,' Alf murmured, and raised his glass, and they all clanked theirs against his. 'She did a marvellous job with raising those grandkids after the accident. And taking Helen on…'

'Here! Here!' said Doug Phillips. James had been seeing him about the diabetic ulcer on his toe.

'Someone had to,' Billy Dingle threw in. Another patient of James—prostate problems. 'Owen wasn't any help.'

'She'll be missed,' said Alf.

There was general agreement around the table.

James stayed on and watched the next game and it was ten o'clock before he got home. He noticed Owen's bike wasn't there. Maybe he'd garaged it?

He expected to see Helen and her father chatting in the lounge room or the kitchen, but the house was quiet, as if it was empty, when he went inside. There were some photo albums scattered on the coffee-table but no other evidence that they'd even been back to the house. Maybe they'd gone to bed. It had, after all, been an emotionally intense day.

As he was passing Helen's room he heard a strange noise. A plaintive whimper like a wounded animal. He raised his hand to knock and then hesitated. What if her father was in there, comforting her? But he couldn't hear any voices. And then the sound came again and it was so mournful he knocked without giving it any further thought.

'Helen?' he said quietly. No response. 'Helen,' he called again, louder this time.

'I'm fine.'

Her muffled answer didn't sound fine. In fact, he was heartily sick of hearing the word. He opened the door. The room was in darkness but the light spilling in from the hallway behind him illuminated her. She was in a black lacy slip, her hair still up, and she was lying in a foetal position, her arms wrapped around her knees. And she was moving slightly.

'I'm fine.'

It was said tonelessly, like a recorded message. Like a pull-the-string doll repeating the same phrase over and over. She didn't look at him, she just stared. She looked frighteningly expressionless.

He advanced slowly into the room. *Where the hell was Owen?* How could he go to bed while his daughter fell apart in the room next door? 'Helen…'

'I'm fine,' she muttered again.

He reached the edge of the bed and then slowly sank to the floor. 'Where's your dad?'

'Gone.'

Gone? 'Gone to bed?'

She gave a harsh laugh, the noise so unexpected that she startled both of them. 'Gone, gone,' she said. 'Left an hour ago. Couldn't stop. Had to go. Too depressing. Too many memories of Mum.'

James stared at her incredulously as she rattled off the words. Owen had left town? His fingers dug into the carpet, fisting in anger. He could feel a flush of heat creep up his neck as a dose of fury flooded into his bloodstream. How could he desert his own flesh and blood like that?

He wanted to leave. Right now. Get on his bike and drag the useless son of a bitch back to town. Demand that he be a father for once. Shake him. Hurt him. Make him suffer as Helen was. Make him see how selfish he was being. Maybe even rearrange that perfect straight smile.

Helen made another low whimpering noise, snapping him out of his vengefulness. He took a deep breath, shocked at the savagery of his response. None of that mattered now. Helen needed him. Helen needed to let go of the grief she'd been burying inside.

'Helen,' he said gently, and placed his hand on her calf. 'It's OK to cry. You need to cry.'

Helen shook her head convulsively. 'No. Elsie wouldn't have wanted me to cry for her.'

James could feel a fine tremor running through the skin beneath his hand. Maybe Elsie wouldn't have—one thing he'd learned out here over the years was that outback women were tough, not prone to emotional tendencies— but he was pretty damn sure Elsie wouldn't want to see Helen like this either. 'Doesn't stop it from hurting, though, does it?'

James felt momentarily lost, he had to get through to her.

'Helen.' He shook her leg. Nothing. 'Look at me, Helen!' He raised his voice and gave her a firm shake. She gasped and looked straight into his eyes.

'You loved Elsie. It's OK to cry and rant and scream and yell. That's what you're supposed to do. You're supposed to beat your chest and shake your fist at the sky. You're allowed to be angry and you're allowed to be sad and you're allowed to want to have your father by your side.'

Helen's eyes filled with hot tears. 'No. I have to keep my chin up.'

James swore. 'No. She raised you, Helen. She's dead. You don't have to keep your chin up. You don't have to do anything you don't want to do.'

He saw a tear spill down her cheek. Felt the trembling beneath his hand intensify, could see her trembling all over as she fought their release.

Another tear fell from the other eye. 'It…it hurts.' Her voice was low, guttural, the admission sounding as if it was wrenched from deep within her.

'Of course it does. When my father died I felt as if my heart had been ripped out of my chest.' And they hadn't even been close. 'It hurts for a long time.'

A sob escaped. 'I don't want to feel this bad any more.'

'It feels worse because you're bottling it up. The pressure's too much. Let it out, Helen. Elsie died. Grieve for her.'

Helen felt overwhelmed by the tide of emotions rising inside her. Her chest hurt, her head hurt, her eyes hurt. She wanted it to stop. She wanted it to be gone. She opened her mouth and released a tiny anguished peep. Like a kitten's meow. And another, more of a moan this time. The moan become a cry, the cry a sob and before she knew it she was blinded by tears and deafened by the noise of the sobs that racked her body.

She didn't feel James moving onto the bed until he was behind her. Pulling her back into him, spooning her, cradling her against his broad chest. She didn't resist, she wasn't capable. It hurt too much inside still and getting rid of it was all that mattered.

The tears came and came, the grief and anguish seemingly inexhaustible. A lifetime of sorrow and heartache falling out at once. She cried not just for Elsie but for years of bottled-up emotion. For her ill mother and for her absent father and an uncertain childhood.

The tears were relentless. Like a tap had been turned on and then broken so it couldn't be turned off. And all the time his chest felt good against her back. Solid. Reassuring. His arm around her waist felt heavy and comforting.

It was a long time before her grief started to wane, her tears started to lessen, her sobs became muted. She slowly became aware of him murmuring soothing words, of his gentle kisses in her hair. She turned in his arms. 'I'm sorry,' she said brokenly, a sob catching her voice.

James rolled on his back and pulled her in close, her body pressed into his side, her head resting against his chest. 'I'm not.'

He stroked her hand which was curled into a fist against his chest. She slowly flattened it and he felt a hard object being pressed into his skin. He lifted her hand and discovered the duck Owen had given her that morning. And he felt another spurt of anger rise in him.

Did her father seriously think it was OK to breeze into town the day she buried probably the most significant person in her life, bearing a mother-of-pearl duck, and then leave again hours later? He removed the object, offended by its symbolism, and placed it on her bedside table. She didn't protest as he'd thought she might and he gently kissed her forehead as he castigated himself for being at the pub when he could have been here with her.

Minutes passed. He lost track of time. He just held her and stroked her arm until her breathing evened out and she slept. Then he slept, too.

Helen awoke in a state of confusion hours later. Her eyes fluttered open and she lay very still, trying to orientate herself. The luminous figures of her alarm clock told her it was twenty past three. Her mouth felt dry and despite her slumber she felt an exhaustion that went deep into her bones. A weariness that came from an emotional rather than a physical source.

Even before the memories came back she knew the solid chest muscles beneath her ear belonged to James. Her nose was pushed against his shirt and she could smell his spicy fragrance. The scent that had been driving her crazy for months. And he was here, on her bed, every magnificent inch of him.

She remembered how he had held her, how he had crooned sweet nothings and kissed her hair. How he had insisted that she let it all go, let it all out. How he had been there for her. How her father had let her down and James had been there to help her through it.

When her father had told her he was going, Helen had been completely shattered. She'd thought he'd stay around for a while, a few days at least. But he had that look in his eye. The one he always got, and she knew any protests would have fallen on deaf ears. She'd needed him to stay but couldn't have borne his rejection. In her fragile state it would have been too much.

The light still spilled in from the hallway and she watched James's face. Relaxed in sleep, it was even sexier. His face was turned away from her slightly and she could just see the shadow at his square jaw and the outline of his full mouth. It pouted deliciously, looking soft and inviting, and then she remembered how hot and hard it could be and she felt heat stir low in her belly.

His chest rose and fell evenly beneath her cheek. Her hand was resting on his stomach and she could feel the tautness of his abs even slackened in slumber. They were warm and solid and she liked the feel of them, liked how, despite his sleep, they reacted slightly as she moved her hand.

Her leg was casually thrown over the top of his thighs. Her own thigh very, very close to his masculinity. All she'd need do was bend her knee a little and she could rub against him. She admired herself against him, her pose possessive. The heat flared in her belly.

Don't do this. You've just buried Elsie, waved goodbye to your father and slobbered all over James like a deranged baby. You're a wreck. You probably look like hell. He's not going to touch you with a bargepole. And, more importantly, you've already told him it wasn't going to happen.

But she wanted to. Suddenly it seemed like a perfectly sensible way to end a really terrible day. She wasn't fooling herself or trying to pretend that he wouldn't be gone in a few weeks. This wasn't about the future. She was a woman, with a woman's needs. This was about tonight. This moment.

Earlier tonight she'd needed to be held and he'd done

that. He'd comforted her as if she'd been a child. But now she needed more. Now she needed to feel like a woman. Not Helen the super-organised practice nurse, or Helen of Helen's Heroes or Helen the recently bereaved. Right now she wanted to be Helen the woman.

Was it going to help her forget a little? Yes. Was it going to help ease the sadness a little? Yes. Was that entirely responsible? No. But did she care? Life was short, the day had been long and harrowing and this was an opportunity she'd already passed up. She was damned if she'd do it again.

Helen lifted her hand from his stomach and advanced it slowly through the air, nervous that he might reject her. Could she stand to be rejected again tonight? Her hand hovered for a second above his jaw before she decided.

His stubble scratched against her finger, sending an erotic shiver down her arm. She traced his jaw, up over the contours of his chin, resting briefly in the indent of his dimple. She reached his lips and stroked her finger along their plump softness.

James woke to the sensation of his lips being caressed. It was light, like a feather, like a whisper. He opened his eyes, shifting slightly to try and assimilate what was happening.

Helen's hand stilled but she didn't remove her finger. She held her breath. Was he awake? His hand slid up and captured hers. He kissed her fingertips lightly and she practically mewed. Then he pulled them away, bringing both their hands down to rest on his chest. He patted her hand soothingly. As if she were a child.

Well, to hell with that.

'You're awake,' she whispered, rising up on her elbow

to look down into his face. His dark hair fell in unruly waves and she wanted to touch it. She moved her hand out from under his and brushed at his fringe.

'Yes.' He smiled, bringing her hand down again.

Helen frowned. In the half-light he looked dark and dangerous, his gypsy soul shining through. She wanted him.

'How are you feeling?' he asked, keeping his voice carefully neutral. Even in the subdued light he could see the flare of the amber flecks in her eyes and he knew he was in trouble. She had lust in her eyes and, as much as he wanted to go there, he didn't think the aftermath of a huge emotional meltdown was an appropriate time.

He was babying her again. She almost said *Horny,* just to get a reaction, but she knew he was just concerned. 'Better,' she admitted.

'Good.'

He looked up into her face and saw the honesty there. But he also saw the passion. He needed to get out. Her leg was very close to the ache in his groin and he knew if he stayed for much longer he might not be responsible for his actions. They'd been right to keep their relationship platonic. Helen was someone who would demand more than he knew how to give. He wouldn't let their resolve falter now.

He swallowed. 'I'd better go.'

Not so fast.

As he made to get up she exerted gentle pressure through her leg and the arm that was slung across his chest. 'No, wait.' She toyed with a button. 'I told you a while back that I wasn't going to act on my attraction to you. And I meant it then. But tonight…tonight I'd like to exercise my female prerogative to change my mind.'

James licked his lips, suddenly very aware of the satiny feel of her slip as it rubbed against him. 'Ah, Helen…I'm not sure that's such a great idea.'

Helen smiled at the struggle she saw going on in his turquoise eyes. 'You don't want to any more?'

He sat up quickly as the line between appropriate and lust blurred, displacing her. He swung his legs over the edge of the bed, keeping his back to her. He couldn't concentrate with her looming over him, her softness pressed into him.

'You've been through an acute emotional upheaval. You're not thinking very clearly.'

'So you do want to?'

'Helen.' He turned slightly to face her, exasperated. 'This isn't about what we want. This is about what's appropriate for the situation.'

She felt like a naughty kid who'd been caught attempting to steal biscuits from the biscuit barrel. *Which may have been OK had she actually got to have a nibble first.* It was time he stopped seeing her as the needy girl of a few hours ago and saw the black-satin-clad woman in front of him. 'I'm not a child, James.'

God, he knew that. She was lying there in black lingerie, looking at him with sin in her eyes. He turned away from her again and ran a harried hand through his hair.

Helen could feel him slipping away from her. Another time she may have admired his self-control but tonight wasn't about control. It wasn't about thinking. Tonight was tactile, not tactical.

She crept up behind him and wound her arms around his neck, pushing her body against him, pressing a kiss to his neck. 'You're not going to make me beg?'

'Helen.'

She loved the warning edge in his voice, the slight crack that told her he was just hanging on. She unwound herself from his neck, slipped off the bed and moved around until she was standing in front of him. Then she knelt between his legs, their heads level.

She moved her face close to his. 'I feel like I've been stripped bare tonight. Emotionally bare. You've seen me at my most vulnerable, my most private. Now I want you to strip me bare physically. I want you to see all of me. You held me before and rocked me and soothed me like you would a child. And I needed that. But I need to feel like a woman now.'

She pressed her lips against his, asking a silent question. There was resistance for a couple of seconds and then he groaned and his mouth softened. And then it opened and his tongue stroked against her lips and she sighed and pressed herself into his body, snaking her arms around his neck and opening her mouth, surrendering it to his.

The long-suppressed passion flared inside her like New Year's Eve fireworks. She moaned and pushed her hands into his hair, wanting, needing to touch him, all of him. Her hands fell to his buttons and her fingers pulled at them impatiently, desperate to feel his naked skin, feeling his heat and needing to get closer.

James could sense her loss of control and pulled away from her mouth, kissing her neck, trying to slow the proceedings down. If she kept going like this, there was no telling how they might end up or how quickly it would all be over.

He'd wanted this for a long time and now they'd thrown caution to the wind, he had no intention of making it less than perfect. And whether she cared to admit it or not, she was still in an emotionally vulnerable state. He wanted this to be slow and easy. Soothing to the ache inside. He wanted it to be thorough, he wanted it to be amazing.

As her hands yanked his shirt out of his trousers and roamed freely over his naked chest and his loins leapt, he knew he had to slow it down. He had to protect her emotional vulnerability. He pulled away from her hot, frenzied mouth.

'Hey, hey, hey,' he crooned, grabbing her hands and bringing them to his mouth, pressing a kiss in each palm. 'Slow down.' He chuckled.

Helen drew in deep ragged breaths, her lips already lamenting the loss of his. 'No,' she croaked.

He laughed again. 'I want this to be perfect. I want to make this right for you. I want it slow and long and gentle. I want to…' he grinned at her '…savour you.'

Helen couldn't believe what she was hearing. Any other time she may have wanted all those things but right now she wanted to feel him inside her more than her next breath.

'Next time,' she whispered, and took his mouth again, revelling in the surge of passion as he met her almost brutal kiss stroke for stroke.

James dragged himself back from the brink of surrender, his erection unbearably tight, straining against its fabric confines. 'Helen,' he moaned into her neck.

Helen drew in some much-needed breaths. He was still treating her with kid gloves. The whole town had been treating her like a fragile piece of china and she was heartily sick of it. 'I'm fine, James. I'm not going to break. I'm not a child.'

'We all need a little tenderness from time to time, Helen.'

She was going to go mad if he didn't take her soon. She needed to prove that she was OK. That she wasn't the grieving girl of hours ago. She was a woman with a woman's appetites.

She pulled out of his arms and stood before him. She whipped her satin slip off over her head and in a second was standing before him in just black lacy knickers. She ran her hand over her naked breasts and watched his pupils dilate.

'Do I look like a child?'

She whipped her undies off, too. 'Do I?'

She pulled her ponytail out and shook her hair free. 'Or do I look like a woman who needs a man?'

James's mouth dried. She was magnificent. Her breasts high and firm, her waist small, her legs slender. Her hair swinging loosely about her shoulders, brushing her delicate collar-bones. The bulge in his pants throbbed with need.

'Because right now I want it rough and hard and fast. Can you give me that?'

He didn't talk, just grabbed her wrist and twirled her around so she landed on the bed on her back under him. He plundered her mouth, all thought of slow and easy totally obliterated. He moved his mouth to a rosy-tipped nipple, savaging it as her hand undid his fly. She pulled his throbbing manhood out of his underpants and squeezed hard. 'Now,' she panted.

She didn't have to ask again. He shed his trousers and was sheathing himself in her hot core seconds later. Her guttural cry spurred him on and he thrust into her again and again, his face at her neck, his hand on her breast.

'Yes. James. Oh, yes.'

He could feel her starting to tighten around him, heard her cries become more desperate, and he rammed into her harder. Faster.

He felt Helen break first, her nails raking down his back. He followed shortly after, joining her in an alternative universe where only their cries and their breath and their rhythm mattered. Not Elsie or Owen. Not their lousy childhoods. Not even his own imminent departure. Just a fantastic, addictive ecstasy which, when they bumped back to earth, left them craving more.

CHAPTER NINE

HELEN woke at seven-thirty the next morning to an empty bed. She still felt exhausted but in a good way. Not weary any more just deeply, deeply sated. James had made love to her again after their first frenzied session. It had been slow and thorough, he had savoured her as he had promised, and she had cried all over again from the sheer beauty of it. And then he had kissed away her tears and they'd fallen asleep together.

She could smell his scent on her sheets, on her pillow, and she knew she wouldn't wash them until it was completely gone. She could also smell coffee. Divine and rich, its earthy fragrance wafting in through her bedroom door. She stretched and felt the protest of internal muscles and blushed, thinking about her aggression.

She lay there for a while, her stomach growling as the aroma of coffee continued to tease her taste buds, her thoughts drifting to James. Was he out there, freaking out? She imagined him pacing, feeling trapped, rehearsing his you-know-I'm-a-gypsy and we-should-just-be-friends speech. She smiled, giving herself a few more minutes before she put him out of his misery.

He was sitting in a lounge chair in his trousers from last night, no shirt, flicking through her albums. He was sipping coffee and for a few seconds she just drank in the sight of him. He looked magnificent. Her toes curled, thinking about the things he had done to her body, the things she'd done to his.

'Hey,' she said.

James looked up. She was standing in the entrance to the room dressed in his shirt. She'd only done up a couple of buttons and he caught a glimpse of creamy breasts, cute belly button and black lacy knickers. Her hair tumbled in disorder, framing her gorgeous face.

His still unsigned contract sat on the coffee-table on top of the pile of albums, taunting him. Seeing her like this, all tousled from bed and his love-making, to sign it seemed like a really stupid idea. He wanted nothing more than to take her hand and spend all day in bed. But he didn't stay. He didn't know how to stay.

'Hey.'

They gazed at each other for a few moments. No words, just hungry looks that throbbed with yearning, desire and lust.

'Coffee smells good,' she said, her voice husky.

'I'll get you a cup.'

He pushed up out of the chair, grateful for something to do other than stare like a horny teenager. His shirt had never looked so damn good.

When he turned around to bring her cup back out to the lounge room she was leaning against the kitchen door-frame. She advanced towards him, her hand extended, and he passed her the mug. She put it down on the bench and pushed herself up and back until she was sitting on the bench beside it.

He remembered how they had shared their first kiss with her sitting on the bench. His gaze zoned in on the generous display of left breast he could now see, including the rosy tip. Dragging his gaze away, it fell to her thighs where the shirt had ridden up to reveal every silky inch. God, she was too underdressed to be sitting like that.

'So,' she said, admiring the muscular definition of his chest. The dainty St Christopher sat in the hollow at the base of his neck.

'So.' He leant against the sink and nodded.

'Are you freaking out about last night?'

That was putting it mildly. 'A little. Are you?'

Helen smiled. 'No.'

James admired her aura of calm. 'O-K.'

'I know what you're thinking. You're thinking, Oh, my God, I took advantage of her in an emotional state, it's not a very honourable thing to do and in the cold light of morning she's going to be upset about it.' She raised an eyebrow at him.

The curve of her breast taunted him, even though he was trying really hard to be a gentleman and not look.

'Something like that.'

'Do I look upset?'

She looked as sexy as hell. She looked like she'd been made love to all night. She looked up for more. 'Not really.'

Helen smiled. 'Right. So get over it. I asked you to do it. In fact, if I remember correctly, I was pretty damn adamant.' She grinned at his grudging smile. 'And it was great. It was just what I needed. So let's just leave it at that. A one-off night that was a great way to end a terrible day.'

He had three weeks left and she really thought that after last night they could live in the same house and not want to repeat the experience? He already wanted her again.

'Really, you shouldn't tell me this is a one-off when you're barely wearing my shirt. In fact, I think we're both a little underdressed for this conversation.'

She grinned at him impishly. 'Do you want it back?'

She was having way too much fun with this. He needed to take back some control here. 'No,' he said, crossing to her, stepping between her thighs, forcing them to part, and reaching for the buttons. He did them all up. Even the top one. 'That's better.' He picked up his mug and headed out of the kitchen.

Helen laughed. 'Speak for yourself.'

She kicked off the bench and followed him, carrying her mug. He was looking through her albums again. She sat opposite him. He was right. If she was trying to convince him this was a one-off then she needed to behave. But she couldn't remember ever feeling this…light. Her weeping last night had purged years' of heartache and it felt good to have it gone.

'You never told me you'd travelled so much.'

She shrugged 'You never asked. In fact, I think you just assumed because I'd lived in Skye all my life that I'd never been anywhere else.'

James nodded. It was true. He had judged her. 'Guilty as charged. I'm sorry.'

'You're forgiven.' After last night she'd have forgiven

him almost anything. 'I guess I inherited a healthy dose of my father's genes.'

He gazed at a photo of a younger Helen, the Eiffel Tower in the background. 'What's your favourite place?'

'Venice.'

He laughed. 'You don't need to think about it?'

She shook her head. 'Nope. There's something special about Venice.'

'Yes,' he agreed, 'there is.'

James flicked through the albums a bit more, the silence between them companionable. Last night had certainly muddied the waters for him. Leaving Skye had become more of a conundrum then it should have been. His wild gypsy soul was calling him on but he knew, like Venice, Helen was special. That there was something special between them. That he wanted to explore what it was. He definitely didn't want to walk away from her.

'Helen…'

She looked up from the fascinating contents of her mug into his serious face. 'James.'

'About last night.'

'Yes.'

'I'm not sure I can live under the same roof and ignore the fact that we had a really incredible night together. Every time I see you I'm going to want to do it again.'

Amen to that. But Helen knew the only way she could wave him goodbye at the end of three weeks and not hang onto his leg as he left like a petulant child was to go cold turkey with the sex.

She shrugged. 'Think of it as a one-night stand. You have had those, haven't you?'

James smiled. 'I've had a couple.'

'There you go. We had a one-night stand. There's no follow-through required.'

James stared at her. *Was she for real?* His erection was almost painful. 'I don't usually see the one-night standee every day, though.'

Helen shrugged again, hoping she looked more nonchalant then she felt. 'We'll manage.'

He raised his eyebrows at her. 'I want you again. Right now.'

Helen felt heat slam into her and it took a few moments to regain the power of speech. 'Look. You're leaving in three weeks. And that's fine. Believe me, if anyone knows about the gypsy soul, it's me. I will stand at this door and wave you goodbye and wish you a good life. But if we spend the next three weeks doing what we did last night, I can't promise I'll be able to do that. If my father leaving last night taught me anything, it's not to settle for less. I will cling. I may cry. I will definitely ask you to stay.'

And I don't want to ask you. I want you to want to.

'Trust me, it will be messy. I'm trying to be mature about this, James. Work with me.'

'What if you came with me?'

Helen froze, her coffee-mug halfway to her mouth. She placed it slowly back on the coffee-table. 'Why?'

'There's something between us, Helen. I don't want to have to say goodbye. I want to be with you. Don't you feel it, too?'

She nodded. 'And yet I haven't asked you to stay. Haven't asked you to do something I know you wouldn't want to do.'

He thrust the photo album on his lap at her. 'I'm not asking you to do something you don't like. You're a traveller, too, Helen. There's gypsy in you. And with Elsie gone, there's nothing holding you in Skye.'

Helen couldn't believe she'd heard him say that. She felt disappointed and angry. Hadn't he been around her long enough to know her? To sense her connection to Skye was about more than a sense of obligation to Elsie? No, he was looking at her blankly, obviously not getting what she was about at all.

But, then, gypsies never did understand the concept of home and what it meant. Her father certainly never had. Her roots were here. Her memories were here. Her soul was here. Yes, she'd travelled. But she liked being grounded and there was no place like home.

'There's never been anything holding me in Skye, James. I choose to stay here.'

He could tell he'd hit a nerve. She was sitting very straight, the sin that had heated the amber flecks in her eyes moments ago frozen out by the rapidly cooling jade. 'So you're just going to live here…for ever?'

She heard the note of incredulity in his voice. That was why it was good he only had three weeks left. Why she'd never ask him to stay. She couldn't live with a man who didn't understand her and always had one eye on the highway out of town. 'Yes. Is that so hard to comprehend?'

For someone who had spent the last five years of his life on his bike or on a plane, or on some kind of transport heading somewhere, yes. 'I guess I just don't understand the urge to be grounded.'

Which wasn't exactly true. Since coming to Skye he'd

felt the most grounded he'd ever been, like he'd found the elusive something he'd been looking for all his life. And as tempting as it was to blame it on the enforced captivity of his broken leg, he knew that was a cop-out. He knew there was something about Helen that grounded him. But he also knew he couldn't give her the things that she deserved.

'You know, life doesn't have to be one or the other, James. You can have the best of both worlds.'

He blinked at the flint in her voice. 'No, Helen, I can't. I chose the gypsy life because I don't have to be beholden to anyone or any place. I grew up trapped in an unhappy house. Powerless to get out. I'm never going to be trapped again.'

Helen stood. She looked down at him, feeling dismay. 'Look, you want to roam around the country for ever, then good luck to you. You want to become Owen then more power to you. There are worse people out there—'

'I'm not sure about that, Helen,' James interrupted. 'What he did last night was unforgivable. I want to hunt him down and kill him and I barely know him. But you're wrong, I don't want to be him. I'll not repeat his mistakes or my parents'. Which is why it's better to keep moving.'

Helen felt tears prick at her eyes. She felt foolishly moved by James's obvious distaste for Owen's disappearing act but she was angry at him, too. He was selling them short.

Fighting with him now, trying to make him see, she knew that she loved him. That she wanted him to stay. It was a really bad time for such a momentous realisation, but her whole body hummed with it.

And it just made this argument even more necessary.

Deep down she knew that they could have a good life together. Things could work and work well because they both had experience to draw on and a determination not to repeat the mistakes of their childhood. Elsie was gone and her father was always going to be a transient figure her in life. But James could be her family. And she could be his. She could make him see that not all relationships were unhappy.

'So you're just going to roam the rest of your life?'

James shrugged. 'Sure.'

'Because you're too scared to stay in one place and give it a try? That's insane, James.'

'I haven't been equipped to nurture a successful relationship. My upbringing didn't teach me how to give emotionally.'

'You did all right with me last night.'

'That's not the same thing, Helen, and you know it.'

'All I know for sure is that you'll never find whatever the hell it is you're looking for until you stop running, James. Do you even know what it is any more?'

Good question. He'd thought he knew but looking at her in his shirt, questioning him, calling him on his beliefs, she was right. What did he want? He'd got away from the sadness of his earlier life but was he any happier? Didn't he want to be happy? To be loved and feel needed? All the things he hadn't had in his younger years.

But what if he stuffed up? What if it didn't work out and he was stuck in Skye in a relationship that was just plain awful? His feelings for Helen were too complicated and, frankly, they scared him. He'd never met a woman who scared him this much.

Helen was someone who would demand everything

from him and he'd been too used to keeping a part of himself back, wary from years of emotional neglect, of not having his feelings returned. It was easier to move on than risk his heart again.

'It's a good life,' he said defensively, as his head roared with conflicting emotions.

'Have you ever thought maybe there's a flipside to your gypsy life that's just as good?'

He'd more than thought it. He'd been living the flipside here in this cottage in Skye with her, and he'd liked it more than he cared to admit.

'I'd hate to stuff up, Helen. I'd hate to hurt you. My past is never far away.'

'Neither is mine, James, but we can't go on like this, forever frightened to live and love and be happy because of what happened decades ago. You know there have been times when I've resented Owen so much. Wished for a proper father, one who was around all the time. I've been disappointed in him and his gypsy lifestyle and his inability to just stay put for a while. But I can't let it—let him—stop me from taking a chance. And you shouldn't let your past mess up a shot at a future either.'

'You don't know how it was,' he said quietly.

'No. Not exactly. But I know it made you sad and that children shouldn't be sad. You had a lousy family.' She shrugged. 'Guess what? So did I. So let's start again. Let's make our own family. Let me be your family.'

James was tempted. Staying here, wrapped up in Helen's arms for ever? Could it be that simple? 'I don't know, Helen.'

She stared at him for a few minutes as her heart broke. If

he didn't know, she was damned if she was going to keep pushing. He had to want this, too. She wasn't going to put her soul on the line, confess her love when he obviously didn't reciprocate. When he still didn't know what he wanted out of life. Because she did know—now. She wanted him.

Helen picked up a pen that was on the coffee-table. 'Then sign the contract,' she said, passing him the pen. 'There's nothing keeping you here.'

And she turned on her heel and stalked into her bedroom before she crumbled in front of him. Her watery eyes scanned the rumpled bed and she just wanted to throw herself on it and cry. *No!* She'd cried enough last night for the rest of her life. No more tears.

James stared after her, pen in hand. How quickly their night of passion and their morning of flirting had vanished when faced with the realities of their very different life-styles. His gaze fell on the contract. She'd painted an attractive picture but he just couldn't visualise how it would work. She deserved to be with someone who could love her with an open heart. Who could see the picture. Who knew how to make it work.

He picked up a pen and signed on the dotted line. She'd thank him for this in the long run.

Courteous was the best way to describe the remaining three weeks of James's locum period. They were polite but distant. A bit like they'd been when their attraction had first flared and she had made it clear that it wasn't going to happen. But it was bleaker than that. He got the impression Helen was marking the days on a calendar.

One with his picture on it.

And a target drawn in felt pen on his head.

He'd tried to approach her the first few days after their argument, tried to explain, but she'd just looked straight through him and said, 'I think we've been over this.'

His body, of course, betrayed him at every turn so her aloofness was a good reminder that they were too different to make things work. The more his body ached for her, the more he craved the open road.

The residents of Skye threw him a farewell party at the CWA hall on his last day of work. Everyone was there. Even Helen. She was tense, her smile forced, but she was there. Alf gave a speech and Josh had made him a poster that said 'Best Doctor in Skye.'

'Are you sure we can't tempt you to stay?' Genevieve asked, rocking a sleeping William as the party flowed around them. 'I don't mind staying on maternity leave. It's going to break my heart to leave him.'

James looked at her guiltily. Looked at the baby he had helped into the world. Looked all around him at the people who had wormed their way into his life with their big hearts and welcoming arms. Each one of them anchored him here.

Maybe he should have checked with Genevieve first. He could have offered to do another four-month stint. But the way things were now with Helen he was relieved to be going. And the road was beckoning him. 'Sorry. I have to be at my next job in a week.'

'That's a shame,' Genevieve mused. 'I kinda thought you and Helen might have…'

James's gaze settled on Helen. She was laughing at something someone was saying. She looked warm and relaxed, so not how she'd been with him, and he found himself yearning for that Helen. 'Ah, no.'

Genevieve nodded. 'Yeah, I guess you're a little too like Owen for her taste.'

James wanted to protest. He wasn't like her father at all. But he supposed, to all intents and purposes, in a lot of ways, he was.

Tom came up and wished him luck, looking more friendly than he ever had. 'Good luck, James,' he said. 'You're going for good, then?'

James clenched his jaw at the smug quality to the paramedic's voice. 'Yes.' The thought of Helen with Tom was more than he could stand. A surge of jealousy ripped through him.

'Well, take care, then. Have a safe trip.'

He moved on and James watched him all the way to the other side of the hall. He turned around and found Helen at his elbow, cuddling William while Genevieve replenished their drinks.

'Promise me you won't settle,' he said to her out the corner of his mouth, smiling at a group of CWA ladies, his gaze still tailing Tom.

'Go to hell, James,' she said sweetly, also smiling at the ladies, and promptly moved away.

Helen lay in bed the next morning, the mouthwatering aroma of brewing coffee wafting into her bedroom. The man she loved was leaving. She wanted to pull the pillow over her head and lock the door.

When it had happened she wasn't sure. Maybe she'd known from their first meeting. Maybe before when an eerie sixth sense had made her uneasy about his delayed arrival. Maybe in some strange, mystical way her soul had sensed the coming of her life partner and her intuition had kicked into overdrive when he hadn't thundered into town on time.

It didn't really matter anyway. The fact was, she did love him. And he was leaving. Which should have been a relief. Loving him and living in the limbo they'd been in the last few weeks was shredding the very fabric of her being. But she wouldn't falter. She'd made it this far without asking him to stay, she sure as hell could make it through a farewell.

It was just such a waste. She'd never been in love before. What on earth had possessed her to fall for an Owen clone she'd never know. A gypsy. She'd get over it, she supposed, eventually, but the loss of what could have been weighed heavily on her as she rose and threw on some clothes. They would have made such beautiful babies.

She padded into the kitchen and he was standing at the sink, his back to her. She headed for the percolator and poured herself a mug. He was dressed in his leather pants and a snug-fitting black T-shirt that hugged the contours of his back and triceps. He didn't turn around.

'When are you off?'

He turned then. 'As soon as I've finished this.'

Her gaze devoured him. The shirt looked just as snug across his chest and his wavy hair brushed his forehead. Her hand shook and her insides performed a series of somersaults. She nodded and looked away, afraid she'd give in despite her resolve. Afraid her body would betray her.

Her legs were shaking as she entered the lounge room and sank into a chair.

He passed behind her a few minutes later, heading to his bedroom. She stared resolutely into her coffee, ignoring him. *I will not ask him to stay. I will not break. I will be fine.*

James re-entered the lounge room. 'I'm off.'

Helen took a mouthful of hot coffee and swallowed it, the heat something to concentrate on other than her breaking heart. She stood. 'OK.'

He walked to the door and she followed, refusing to acknowledge how hot he looked in his leathers. He opened the door and turned to face her. She'd been quite close behind him so consequently they were now very close indeed.

'Guess this is goodbye,' he said softly.

Helen nodded as she watched his mouth form the words. His lips were soft and perfect.

He watched as her ponytail swished from side to side. He was going to miss that ponytail. A silence stretched between them. 'Thank you…for everything. I'm sorry for—'

Helen cut him off, placing two fingers against his lips. Mainly because she couldn't bear to hear it. But also because his lips were so damn irresistible and it'd be the last time she touched them. 'Shh. No,' she whispered. 'Let's not rehash things. Let's just say goodbye and leave it at that.'

His lips tingled where she'd touched them. He wanted her so much. 'Helen…'

His voice was rough, halfway between a whisper and a groan. His lips grazed erotically against the pads of her fingers. She felt a pull down low and was helpless to resist the power of his mouth.

She met his lips with a passion that he equalled and then

intensified. He stabbed his fingers into her hair as he plundered the softness of her mouth and yanked the band from the ponytail. He stroked his fingers against her scalp and her freed hair fell loosely around her shoulders. His lips stoked the furnace that had been smouldering for weeks and her heart hammered even as it broke.

Helen pulled away, breathing hard, knowing this was madness. Her head fell against his chest, his lips against her hair.

James held her tight. 'Ask me to stay.'

Tears pricked her eyes as his voice rumbled through his chest and vibrated into her ear. *Stay*. She looked up at him. 'No, you have to want to.'

James felt torn. He wanted to. He did. But the chains of his past were too heavy to shake. 'Helen.'

She heard the plea in his voice but saw the indecision in his turquoise gaze. She shook her head and stepped away from him. 'Just go, James.'

James opened his mouth to say more. But she was standing there with her arms wrapped around her waist, aloof again. He nodded, picked up his backpack and walked out the door.

Helen stared after him for a moment then slowly shut the door. She leaned her forehead against the wood as the sound of his vintage Harley broke the air.

'Stay,' she whispered.

It wasn't until James pulled into a roadside hotel that evening that he realised he'd been looking back all day. He never looked back. His jumbled thoughts and his heavy heart were yearning for Skye. For Helen.

Hell. He loved her. Even as his heart lifted, the thought depressed the hell out of him. This had not been in his plans. He stared at the telephone beside the bed. His fingers itched to ring her. Hear her voice.

What a stubborn fool he'd been. His heart beat loudly at the thought of a future with her. It scared the hell out of him. But a future without her scared him more. She'd asked him to be her family and he'd turned her down. What an A-grade fool!

It was four a.m. when James made it back to Skye. Suppressing the urge to barge into the house, knowing the door would be unlocked, he knocked.

Helen woke with a start.

'Open up, Helen. It's James.'

She stumbled through the house, her hammering heart matching the rapping on the door, beat for beat.

James stared impatiently at the stubbornly shut door. 'Damn it, Helen!'

She reached for the latch and yanked it open. 'Are you trying to wake up the whole neighbourhood?' she hissed.

He opened his mouth to say something else and she grabbed his arm and dragged him inside the house. 'It's four in the morning James.'

She was wearing *that* sleep shirt and her hair was loose and he wanted her so badly he had to shove his hands into the pockets of his leather jacket to stop from reaching for her.

'I love you,' he said. 'I don't know how I'll go or if it will work but you asked me earlier what I was looking for and it took leaving you to realise that I've been looking for you. Someone to help heal the sadness of my past, someone to make a better future with. Together. I've felt more wanted and needed and at home here in Skye than I've ever felt anywhere. And that's because of you, Helen. I knew you were different from the day you pulled me out of the bush. I've just been too busy running scared to see what was right in front of my nose.'

Helen felt a jumble of emotions tumble around inside her as James stood before her, laying his soul bare. Was she dreaming? Love, hope and triumph clashed inside her. Still she didn't dare hope.

'But what about the gypsy rider? What about the freedom of the open road?' She needed to be sure.

'You were right, Helen. I've been running away. I didn't take up the travelling life because it's in my blood, although I've loved it…but because I was afraid of commitment. Afraid of loving someone and not being loved back again. Is it too late to take you up on the offer of being a family? Please, tell me you love me. Please, tell me I haven't blown it before it even had a chance to begin.'

He looked so forlorn standing in her lounge room in his bikie leathers. And he loved her. But still she held out.

'What about kids?'

James expelled a heavy breath. *Children?* The thought was almost as terrifying as loving her and being together for ever. 'You want kids?'

Helen nodded. 'Of course. What about you?' She held her breath—neither of them had had great childhoods. Bringing children into the world was big for both of them.

The amber in her eyes glittered like fiery embers. She was magnificent and he suddenly realised he wanted the whole catastrophe. Even kids, yes. With her…yes. He did. It was daunting but he knew that with them as parents their kids were going to be doted on and loved and the most wanted children on the planet.

He smiled. 'Yes.'

He hadn't been prepared for this. For her. For how grounding love could be. How you wanted to stay when you found that one special person. How you wanted everything. The whole box and dice. But he was damn glad he had.

Helen trembled with the urge to put her arms around him but she needed him to be sure. 'So you think a guy with commitment issues and a girl with abandonment issues can make a go of it? It doesn't sound like a very auspicious start.'

He shrugged and smiled. 'We'll reinvent the wheel.' He looked at the smile that spread across her face and felt encouraged. 'Well? Come on, Helen, you're killing me here. Do you love me too?'

Helen nodded, feeling overwhelmed suddenly by events.

James reached for her and pulled her hard against him. 'Oh, thank you. Thank you, thank you,' he whispered, pressing kisses all over her face. 'I'm never letting you go.'

Helen laughed. She hadn't felt this light, this giddy in weeks. 'I love you James.'

He smiled down into her happy face. 'I'm so sorry—'

'No,' Helen said, placing her fingers on his lips. 'No looking back. We're reinventing the wheel, remember.'

The curve of her bottom felt good snuggled into his palms and he nodded.

'Stay,' she whispered.

James grinned. 'I thought you'd never ask.'

And he dipped his head, sealing their love with a kiss.

EPILOGUE

IT WAS a beautiful day in Skye when James and Helen wedded three months later. The CWA hall was decorated with yellow wattle flowers, white ribbons and pink balloons. A local band played rock and roll tunes on the stage as the entire population partied with the newlyweds.

Helen sat next to her father and watched her new husband pound the wooden floorboards with an energetic Josh. A bright blue cast covered the five-year-old's newly broken arm. But it hadn't stopped him from wearing the cute little white tuxedo or from relinquishing the white satin ring cushion he'd carried proudly down the aisle.

'He's a good man, darling.'

She smiled at her father. 'I know.' She squeezed his hand.

Owen looked down into his daughter's flushed face. He'd never seen her looking prettier. 'I'm so sorry, Helen. I haven't been a very good father.' He raised his hand and grazed his knuckles lightly down her cheek. 'You're so like your mother. She would have been so proud. Elsie would have been, too.'

Helen covered her father's hand with her own and gave him a gentle smile. For all his failings, she'd always known he'd done his best. 'Thanks, Dad.'

'Come on, dance with your old man.' He stood and held out his hand.

Helen gathered her voluminous skirt and took her father's hand. The band played a jive tune and her father spun her round the floor.

'Excuse me.' James tapped Owen on the shoulder. 'I'd like to dance with my wife.'

Helen melted into her husband's arms as the music slowed to a waltz.

'Are you happy, my darling?' James asked.

'More than I ever imagined possible,' Helen sighed looking into his amazing turquoise eyes. 'What about you? Are you glad you came back?'

James kissed her nose. 'More than you'll ever know.' And he pulled her close and waltzed the night away with the woman of his heart.

MILLS & BOON®

MEDICAL™

proudly presents

Brides of Penhally Bay

Featuring Dr Nick Tremayne

A pulse-raising collection of emotional, tempting romances and heart-warming stories — devoted doctors, single fathers, Mediterranean heroes, a sheikh and his guarded heart, royal scandals and miracle babies…

Book Seven

SINGLE DAD SEEKS A WIFE

by Melanie Milburne

on sale 6th June 2008

A COLLECTION TO TREASURE FOREVER!
One book available every month

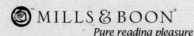

Celebrate 100 years
of pure reading pleasure
with Mills & Boon®

To mark our centenary, each month we're publishing a special 100th Birthday Edition. These celebratory editions are packed with extra features and include a FREE bonus story.

Plus, starting in February you'll have the chance to enter a fabulous monthly prize draw. See 100th Birthday Edition books for details.

Now that's worth celebrating!

15th February 2008

Raintree: Inferno by Linda Howard
Includes FREE bonus story Loving Evangeline
A double dose of Linda Howard's heady mix of passion and adventure

4th April 2008

The Guardian's Forbidden Mistress by Miranda Lee
Includes FREE bonus story The Magnate's Mistress
Two glamorous and sensual reads from favourite author Miranda Lee!

2nd May 2008

The Last Rake in London by Nicola Cornick
Includes FREE bonus story The Notorious Lord
Lose yourself in two tales of high society and rakish seduction!

Look for Mills & Boon 100th Birthday Editions at your favourite bookseller or visit
www.millsandboon.co.uk

0108/CENTENARY_2-IN-1

FREE

4 BOOKS AND A SURPRISE GIFT!

We would like to take this opportunity to thank you for reading this Mills & Boon® book by offering you the chance to take FOUR more specially selected titles from the Medical™ series absolutely FREE! We're also making this offer to introduce you to the benefits of the Mills & Boon® Reader Service™—

- ★ **FREE home delivery**
- ★ **FREE gifts and competitions**
- ★ **FREE monthly Newsletter**
- ★ **Books available before they're in the shops**
- ★ **Exclusive Reader Service offers**

Accepting these FREE books and gift places you under no obligation to buy; you may cancel at any time, even after receiving your free shipment. Simply complete your details below and return the entire page to the address below. You don't even need a stamp!

YES! Please send me 4 free Medical books and a surprise gift. I understand that unless you hear from me, I will receive 6 superb new titles every month for just £2.99 each, postage and packing free. I am under no obligation to purchase any books and may cancel my subscription at any time. The free books and gift will be mine to keep in any case.

M8ZEE

Ms/Mrs/Miss/Mr.....................................Initials ....

BLOCK CAPITALS PLEASE

Surname ....

Address ....

....

....Postcode ....

Send this whole page to:

The Reader Service, FREEPOST CN81, Croydon, CR9 3WZ